"This tense w_____ s_____

_____ _____, with attractive characters,
fast-paced plot and a feel good finale."
Daily Mail

"A real page turner, valuable for reviving the reading
experience of any jaded sports fans. They'll love it
for the insight and info into Premier League footie
alone, and, as the real hook, probably think . . .
if only it were me."
Books for Keeps

"Brilliantly paced football excitement
on and off the pitch in this fast moving adventure."
Lovereading4kids (Julia Eccleshare)

"A cracking read . . . everyone will be swept up
in the action thriller."
School Librarian

"A gripping read for soccer fans."
Irish Examiner

"A satisfying wish-fulfilment epic."
Jewish Chronicle

"Nat's emotions are believable, and came across
loud and clear. There were plenty of
edge of the seat moments."

Text copyright © Jonny Zucker 2011
The right of Jonny Zucker to be identified as the author of this
work has been asserted by him in accordance with the Copyright,
Designs and Patents Act, 1988 (United Kingdom).

First published in Great Britain in 2011 by
Frances Lincoln Children's Books, 4 Torriano Mews,
Torriano Avenue, London NW5 2RZ
www.franceslincoln.com

A catalogue record for this book is available from the British Library.

ISBN 978-1-84780-079-4

Printed in Croydon, Surrey, UK by CPI Bookmarque Ltd.
in June 2011

1 3 5 7 9 8 6 4 2

STRIKER BOY
KICKS
OUT

Jonny Zucker

F

FRANCES LINCOLN
CHILDREN'S BOOKS

CHAPTER 1
Passport Fear

The heat and humidity of the Spanish night hit Nat as he stepped out of the plane. He loosened his vertical green-and-white striped Hatton Rangers Football Club tie, and walked down the steps. It was three years since he'd last visited Spain, but this trip would be very different from that time.

A ripple of excitement unfolded inside him.

"Keep moving, lads," shouted Stan Evans, the Rangers assistant manager. Nat strolled across the tarmac to the terminal building with his two best mates – tall central-defender Emi Adeyo and right-back Kelvin Bartlett.

They passed through the sliding glass doors of the terminal building, climbed two flights of stairs and walked down a long corridor – its walls covered with Spanish flags.

At passport control, Nat hung back with Stan as planned. When everyone else had gone through, Nat and Stan deliberately approached a female customs official, in the hope that she'd be less likely to follow football than her male colleagues. Evans explained to her in basic Spanish that Nat was a youth team player who had come along for the experience. She held out her hand.

Nat unzipped his jacket pocket and handed over his passport. He gulped nervously as she checked his face against the photo. It showed a boy with light green, almond-shaped eyes, a snub nose and an l-shaped dimple on his chin. His hair was closely cropped, a marked change from the long mane he'd sported until he'd joined Rangers.

The official looked from the photo to Nat and back again. His insides doubled over in anxiety. Was she a football fan who followed the English Premier League? Had she recognised him from his three appearances as a substitute? The wait was agonising, but finally she stamped the relevant page and arched an eyebrow for him to proceed. He walked through quickly, relief coursing through him, slipped the passport back into his pocket and refastened the zip.

It was critical that none of the other Rangers players ever saw Nat's passport. To them, he was Nat Dixon, a sixteen-year-old professional footballer. His passport, however, told a different story. It revealed that his real name was Nat Cartwright. And that he was only thirteen.

The only people who knew the truth were Nat and his father Dave, Stan Evans, and Hatton Rangers manager Ian Fox.

"Well done," said Evans, his clear blue eyes smiling with satisfaction, his steps affected by his slight limp, as he rejoined Nat after being waved through. They hurried to catch up with the rest of the Rangers party.

"You alright, mate?" asked Neil 'the Wildman' Duffy, the club captain, when he saw Nat approach. The Wildman was the sort of player anyone would wish for in the heart of their defence – built like a mountain, with an apparently endless supply of strength and bravery.

"Yeah," responded Nat, placing a protective hand over his jacket pocket and the passport inside.

"Good," replied the Wildman. "Although I'm warning you, getting back into training will be a shock to your system. You'll feel your joints groaning tomorrow night."

Nat smiled. This was typical of the Wildman – he told things as they were, without intending to frighten or undermine anyone. It was one of the qualities Nat liked best about him.

It was hard to believe that the last game of the season, a three-two victory over Manchester United which had saved the club from relegation thanks to Nat's last-minute strike – had been just three weeks ago. Nat and the rest of the Rangers players had expected to turn up at Shelton Park, the Rangers training ground, for the first session of pre-season training this morning, yet here they were in Spain. Life could deliver great surprises.

"Look sharp, lads!" called Ian Fox, marshalling his

troops in the direction of the baggage reclaim carousels. Fox, with his black hair streaked with grey, his sharp, angular nose and thin lips, could look and act harshly, at the best of times. But he was a good man, you just had to try not to get on his bad side – something Nat had done in the past, to his regret.

Twenty minutes later, everyone had their luggage and they walked out into the pale yellow lights of the arrivals lounge. Several people stood behind a metal barrier holding up placards. A man in a dark blue suit with a chauffeur's hat held a sign reading HATTON RANGERS. A woman in an orange skirt and top held up a piece of cardboard with the word ADEYO, and a small, nut brown man with wispy grey hair had a piece of paper marked BARTLETT. Further down stood a young man of about seventeen, with dark brown eyes and long brown hair that was held in place by a thin black headband stretching across his forehead. His features were flat, as if someone had hammered them into place. The sign he was holding read DIXON.

"Your carriage awaits you," said Stan Evans, nodding in the direction of Nat's sign. "Get a decent night's sleep and we'll see you in the morning."

Nat nodded and went over to Emi and Kelvin to say goodbye. As the three youngest players in the squad, they'd been given the short straw when it was discovered that the hotel the club had booked couldn't accommodate the entire squad.

"I can't believe we miss out on the hotel," sighed Kelvin.

"Don't worry," said Emi, "we'll still be spending loads of time there."

They all shook hands and headed off to their respective greeters.

Nat's Spanish adventure was about to begin.

CHAPTER 2
Night Welcome

"Hi," said Nat.

"I'm José," replied the boy. "Welcome to Andalusia. You'll be staying with my mother and me. Shall I take your bag?"

"I'm alright, thanks."

"The car's just outside," said José, leading the way.

Nat took a quick look over his shoulder and saw Emi and Kelvin heading off with their hosts, and the rest of the Hatton Rangers party clambering onto a large coach. Nat followed José out of the building. They turned left and walked to a short-stay parking bay. José took Nat's suitcase and dropped it onto the back seat of an old and battered green ex-army jeep. He motioned for Nat to climb into the front passenger seat.

The jeep roared away from the parking bay, past the Hatton Rangers coach. They drove down a long road that ended in a T-junction. The signpost pointing left read ALMERÍA. The one pointing right said TALORCA/ MÁLAGA.

José turned right. The road curved to the left, and after a few minutes, Nat spotted the inky-black waters of the Mediterranean Sea on his left. On his right was dry open land covered in the silhouettes of evergreen trees – one of the only types of foliage that could withstand the baking, rain-starved summer months of Andalusia.

"It's good of you to have me to stay," said Nat.

"No problem," replied José, his eyes firmly on the road.

"How was it arranged?" asked Nat. "Are you connected to Talorca FC?"

José nodded.

"What's the connection?"

"My father used to work for them."

"Cool," nodded Nat. "Are you into football?"

"It's OK," responded José, with a shrug of his shoulders.

"Are you a Talorca fan?"

José shrugged again.

"Do you ever go to matches?"

José moved his head a fraction, though whether this was a nod or a shake of the head was impossible to fathom.

OK, thought Nat, *so José isn't the world's number one conversationalist.*

The road curved left again until they were driving right beside the sea. Nat smelt the salty freshness of the water. In the distance ahead he saw the silhouetted outlines of a city skyline. But before they approached Talorca's outskirts, José took a right, away from the sea, and onto a much smaller road that climbed a steep hill. They drove through a vast olive grove, the jeep's tyres kicking up clouds of dust in its wake. When they reached the brow of the hill, José sped down the other side and applied the brakes as they reached the bottom, next to a small whitewashed villa.

A compact red Fiat was parked beside a fence. There was a courtyard to the right of the villa, containing a small pear tree, a wrought-iron bench and a basketball hoop attached to one of the walls. On the far side of the courtyard was a dilapidated wooden shack with a sloping corrugated plastic roof punctured with holes.

José climbed out of the jeep, grabbed Nat's suitcase from the back seat and walked towards the front door, with Nat following behind.

They went inside and Nat found himself in a small entrance way, the floor of which was covered in shoes, old tennis rackets, a fishing rod, piles of fashion magazines and an assortment of hats, hanging on a thin oak hatstand. In front of him was a corridor with a series of rooms leading off it on both sides. Paintings of flowers in bold bright colours adorned the corridor walls.

To his right was a small passageway, and it was from a door at the end of this that a woman appeared, wiping her hands on her apron and smiling broadly. She was wearing a flowing emerald green dress and had long, curly brown hair, which was tied back in a ponytail. Her sparkling eyes matched her dress, and her narrow features were very similar to José's.

"Hello Nat," she said warmly, offering him her hand, which he shook. "I'm Inés, and you've obviously met my son José." Her English was spoken with only the barest trace of an accent.

José put Nat's suitcase on the ground, said something to his mother in Spanish and walked off down the corridor, disappearing into the second room on the left.

"It's lovely to have you here," smiled Inés. "I'll show you around and then we'll eat supper, or *cena*, as we call it."

Nat had picked up a bit of Spanish on his travels and was keen to learn more. He took hold of his suitcase and the tour commenced. Inés pointed out the bathroom and her bedroom, the first on the left of the main corridor, the second facing it. The doors to these rooms were open so he took a quick look inside as they passed. Inés's room was neat but sparsely furnished, with a bed, a wooden dresser and a wardrobe. The bathroom had a simple shower and a sink. José's bedroom was next on the left but his door was firmly shut and angry chords from a Spanish heavy rock band spilled out from under his door. Facing that was a small office with a desk and a computer. The last room on the left was a toilet, and facing that was another bedroom.

"This is your room," declared Inés, opening the door.

It was a square-shaped space, housing a single bed next to a latticed window, a tall cupboard, a small writing desk and a pile of old board games on the floor. Inés opened the cupboard door. It was empty inside.

"We want you to feel at home here," she smiled. "Please arrange the room however you wish."

"It's fine like this," replied Nat, parking his suitcase next to the bed and dropping his wallet and keys onto the desk.

"Can I ask you a question?" he said.

"Of course."

"How come your English is so good?"

Inés laughed. "I'm an English teacher," she replied. "It doesn't pay very well but I absolutely love it. I teach Spanish teenagers to speak and write your language. Some of them are good learners, while others are better at looking out of the window. We're in the middle of the school holidays at the moment. Having you stay here is a great opportunity for me to practise my own English with a genuine Englishman!"

Nat laughed.

"Get comfortable and come to the kitchen for something to eat in, say, half an hour?" said Inés.

"Sounds great," nodded Nat.

When Inés left, Nat lay down on the bed and shut his eyes. Once again he thought about the unbelievable situation he found himself in. He was thirteen but he'd already appeared three times as a Hatton Rangers substitute, and these hadn't been insignificant games. They'd been high-octane, Premier League matches against Tottenham, Liverpool and Manchester United. Nat still had to remind himself that being part of the Rangers set-up was real. Some mornings he woke up expecting to discover the whole thing had been part of an elaborate dream. But it wasn't. It was really happening. And more than anything else, he wanted to keep it going for as long as was humanly possible.

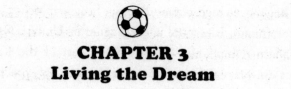

CHAPTER 3
Living the Dream

It had all started because of an incredible piece of luck.

Nat and his father, Dave, had been at a Hatton Rangers 'in the Community Day'. Nat had been playing a superb cameo role in a five-a-side match when Stan Evans happened to be passing. The Rangers assistant manager had been blown away by Nat's speed and the ferocity of his shooting. Rangers were in deep trouble at the bottom of the Premier League. Evans saw amazing potential in Nat, just from those five short minutes, but he'd been very disappointed to discover that, despite Nat's size and maturity, he was only thirteen, and so could be of no use to the team.

But when Evans told Rangers manager Ian Fox about this 'wonderkid', the two of them hatched a plan. Nat and his father had been out of the country for seven years and had broken off all contact with anyone they'd ever known in the UK. So no one knew them, or knew that they were back.

This meant that Hatton Rangers could tell the world

that Nat was sixteen, making him eligible to play for Rangers. It was mad. It was risky. But it might just work.

Dave had initially been dead set against this plan, but Nat had finally won him round.

So Nat had finished the season as a Hatton Rangers player, in addition to thwarting a massive match-fixing scam involving the Hatton Rangers goalkeeper Chris Webb. It had been a quite remarkable few months.

Nat had fed the story of his involvement with the match-fixing scam as an exclusive to journalist Ray Swinton, which stopped Swinton from running a piece raising questions about Nat's real age. Not that Nat trusted Swinton to keep quiet about this forever – after all, he was a journalist. And none of this stopped Nat from constantly worrying that one day he'd be found out. Sometimes this worry lurked in the deeper recesses of his mind, but at other times it was right out there at the front, screaming loudly.

As Nat lay on the bed, mulling all of this over, he must have dozed off, because the next thing he knew was a knock on his bedroom door. He opened his eyes, got off the bed and opened the door.

It was Inés. "*Cena* awaits," she smiled.

Nat followed her back down the corridor, along the narrow passageway and through the door leading into the kitchen. The first thing that hit him was the incredible smell. It made him realise how hungry he was. He'd eaten lunch hours ago with Dave at their cottage. All he'd had since then was a small packet of nuts on the plane.

The kitchen was rectangular, with an Aga-type oven and a large map of Spain on the far wall.

"Please, sit down," said Inés, pouring Nat a glass of thirst-quenching lemonade. She opened the door and called José's name. A minute later he walked into the kitchen, taking his place opposite Nat.

"OK," announced Inés. "We have *pescado frito* – that's fried fish." She placed a large bowl containing a mountain of fish pieces, fried to perfection, on the table. "And this is *ajoharina* and *ensalata mixta* – potatoes in garlic sauce and salad. Please eat what you want and leave what you don't."

Nat nodded his thanks, served himself some of the fish and potatoes and passed the bowls on to José and Inés. It all tasted delicious.

"So why did Everton pull out of the tournament?" asked Inés, pouring herself some lemonade.

"Lots of their players caught some kind of virus," answered Nat, wiping his mouth on a napkin. "Talorca FC wanted Newcastle to replace them but they couldn't make it either, so they contacted Hatton Rangers, literally at the last minute. I only got the call a few hours before we had to be at the airport."

Nat glanced sideways at José who was spearing a piece of fish on his fork. He wore an expression on his face that didn't indicate whether he was interested in this conversation or not.

"So there are two leagues for the tournament?" asked Inés.

Nat nodded. "We're in a mini-league with Lazio and Celtic. Talorca are in the other league with Hamburg and Marseilles. Each team plays the other teams in their league. The winners of the two leagues play each other in the final on Saturday."

"Talorca will get through," observed José, taking a sip of lemonade from his glass. "They've spent a huge amount of money in the last couple of years. It's like Chelsea in your Premier League – they've *bought* themselves success."

"You're so right!" nodded Nat enthusiastically, pleased to find something that he and José agreed on.

"I follow Talorca and Spanish football avidly," said Inés, "but I'm not very familiar with the English Premier League – I apologise for that. But from the information Talorca emailed me, I know you're sixteen and that you're a striker?"

"Yeah," replied Nat. "But I'm very new at the club. They signed me before the transfer window closed back in January, but there were problems with the paperwork so I only got to join up with the team a few months ago."

This was the line Stan Evans and Ian Fox had invented for Nat. He could recite it in his sleep.

"He's being modest," cut in José. "He scored the winning goal against Manchester United on the last day of the season. He saved Hatton Rangers from being relegated. That's a big deal. There are some people in England who think Nat may be 'the next big thing'."

"I don't know about that," blushed Nat. "It'll take me a few years to prove myself."

"It sounds like you're doing pretty well already," smiled Inés, "and as the club have given us tickets for both of your league games we'll be able to see for ourselves. They've also invited us to the Lazio versus Celtic game."

Nat's cheeks went even redder.

José said something sharply to his mother in Spanish.

"Alright," she replied, quickly changing the subject. "Have you been to Spain before?"

"I spent a month in Barcelona about three years ago," Nat replied. "My dad and I travelled for quite a long time. That was one of our stops. We saw a game at Camp Nou. It was awesome!"

"How long were you away for?" enquired Inés.

"Seven years," responded Nat.

"*Seven?*" exclaimed Inés in astonishment.

"I was . . . I was . . . nine when we set out," responded Nat, who'd learned to add three years to every stage of his life, to make sure his fabricated backstory held tight.

Inés was about to ask another question when the phone rang and she went to answer it. Nat and José sat in silence. Nat thought about attempting to follow up the comments about clubs buying success, but José stood up, walked to the sink, placed his plate in it and left the room. Nat watched him go, unable to work him out. Was he shy or unfriendly, hostile or disinterested? As Inés continued her call, Nat went to the sink and started on the washing-up.

A couple of minutes later, Inés wrapped up her call. "You're a guest. You don't need to do that!" she said, wagging a reproachful finger at Nat, as if he was one of her students.

"It's no big deal," replied Nat.

"Well, OK then," she laughed, taking a tea towel and doing the drying-up. When they'd finished, Inés beckoned Nat over to the map of Spain on the wall. "How much do you know about Spanish geography?" she enquired

"Er . . . a little."

"We're about three miles outside of Talorca," she said, placing a finger on the map, "and a mile and a half from the sea. Up the coast is Almería, down the coast is Málaga, and a bit further on is that favourite resort of the British – Marbella. You said you've been to Barcelona? Well, there it is up on the north-east, beside the Balearic Sea. Madrid, of course, is pretty much bang in the centre of the country."

Nat studied the map and took in some of the place names. As well as Barcelona and Real Madrid, there were several other top flight Spanish teams who played regular Champions League football – Sevilla, Málaga and, more recently, Talorca themselves.

And José had been right about large amounts of money being pumped into Talorca FC. Their millionaire President, Victor Mabena, had poured a fortune into the club. In the last couple of seasons, Talorca FC had signed some world-class players – especially their number ten, Lombardo, a Brazilian who possessed a mesmerising collection of tricks and skills. Their captain Alberto Tieras, originally from Bilbao, had been snapped up from AC Milan, also for a substantial sum. And he'd been worth it – terrorising attackers with his trademark 'no-nonsense' tackles.

"I'm sure you'll get used to the weather quite quickly," said Inés, "but the days will be far hotter than back home. And even though you'll have your meals at the standard English times here, we Spanish eat lunch and supper much later than you. So don't be surprised if you're offered food at all sorts of different times!"

"Thanks for the warning!"

Inés yawned. "I need to get some rest," she smiled. "I'll drop you off at training after breakfast."

"Really?" asked Nat, who hadn't thought about the logistics of staying elsewhere from the rest of the team.

Inés nodded. "I'll say goodnight now," she said, before leaving the kitchen and heading for her bedroom.

Nat walked to a door on the other side of the kitchen which led to the courtyard and stepped outside. It was just after 11 p.m. and it was still warm, even though a faint breeze blew across the courtyard. The black sky was lit up by thousands of stars. Nat strolled over to the large shed he'd seen earlier. Its door was wedged open and shafts of moonlight shone through. Nat poked his head inside and spotted several pieces of broken farm machinery, a smashed-up motorbike and piles of logs.

He was about to go back inside when his mobile rang.

"Nat."

"Hi Dad, how's it going?"

"Good. How was your flight?"

"Easy."

"And the place you're staying?"

"Really comfortable. Nice people – a woman and her son."

"Look, mate, I'm really sorry, but I won't be able to make it out for either of your group games. Work's really mad. I've got to build this massive bookcase and some shelving units."

"No problem," replied Nat, attempting to cover his disappointment. "I'm really tired so I'm heading off for bed now."

"Good idea, mate."

"Speak to you soon."

"Of course, sleep well."

Nat went back indoors, changed into his pyjamas and went to the bathroom to brush his teeth. He was upset that his dad wouldn't be able to make the matches. He always felt better when Dave was in the crowd. Mind you, if his dad had got *his* way Nat would have already started at secondary school and be facing a new term in a few weeks time. The Rangers adventure would have never happened. Instead, Nat was out here in Spain, having broken into playing for the Rangers first team, and approaching a major pre-season football tournament.

With this delicious thought floating through his mind, he fell into a deep slumber.

CHAPTER 4
Break-out

An hour after Nat fell asleep, the supper shift at Adelcia Prison was drawing to a close. Situated fifteen miles from Talorca's La Plaza Stadium, the prison had a reputation for being very tough. Even the most hardened criminals picked up new skills here. A guard named Parerra was standing at the front of the prisoners' queue, while the other guard, Haldas, waited at the back. In Parerra's hands was a small electronic device. On its screen were the names of each prisoner present. They were lining up in the canteen. Parrera viewed the queue and ticked off each of the twenty names on the screen. A prisoner named Carlos was at the very back of the line. His cellmate Mundo was three places in front of him. Carlos was tall and wiry, with spiky hair and dark brown eyes. An earring in the shape of a sword hung from his right ear, a tattoo of a dragon perched on the back of his neck. Mundo was short and squat, with small, suspicious eyes and a mane of thick black hair. He walked with a swagger and had a perpetual hacking cough.

Carlos and Mundo's cell was small and uncomfortable.

All it contained were bunk beds with two thin mattresses, two prison regulation blankets, a small sink, a tiny table and two chairs.

"OK, let's go!" barked Parerra.

The men moved towards a door at the far side of the canteen. This was covered by a metal grille and had three locks. Parerra pulled out a bunch of keys and slowly undid the locks. The prisoners started to file through.

"Hurry up!" shouted Parerra.

Carlos watched everything intensely, his entire body poised for action.

"Come on, you lot!" shouted Haldas from the back.

At that second, Mundo cried out in pain.

Parerra waited at the front of the queue, and held up his hand for the prisoners to stop. Haldas suspiciously hurried towards Mundo, who was bent double.

"I think it's my appendix," groaned Mundo.

Haldas had seen a lot of prisoners pretending to be in pain before and he unleashed his baton, prepared in case Mundo tried to jump him. But when he reached the prisoner his suspicions instantly evaporated. This looked like the real thing. Mundo seemed to be in genuine agony.

"Call medical!" shouted Haldas.

Parerra quickly looked down at his trouser pocket to pull out his walkie-talkie.

This glance took three seconds but it was all Carlos needed.

Parerra retrieved his walkie-talkie and instructed the

medical team to meet them at Mundo's cell. Haldas eased Mundo up, put an arm round his shoulders and shouted for Parerra to lead on. Parerra gave him a thumbs-up and continued ushering the prisoners out of the canteen. Mundo was writhing in pain as Haldas led him forwards. Parerra waited until the prisoners were through, then closed the three locks and proceeded down the corridor.

What neither Haldas nor Parerra noticed was that there were now only nineteen prisoners.

Carlos had disappeared.

In that crucial three seconds, Carlos had silently backed away from the line and slipped over the serving counter that fronted the prison kitchen. He crouched down and slipped unseen past two cooks who were busy arguing over a large pot. He exited by some swing doors at the back. This led him to a long corridor which arched to the right. He hurried down this and reached a metallic green door. A panel with number keys stood on the wall. He pressed a sequence of numbers and the door clicked open.

He was now in the tarmac courtyard at the front of the prison. The high brick walls were topped with large coils of razor wire. Only a fool would try and get over them. Carlos hung back in the shadows. He scoured the area for a sign of Bellos, the guard he'd bribed heavily for assistance, but there was no sign of him. Carlos felt his muscles clenching in anxiety. Mundo (who had also been paid) had bought him time in the canteen with an excellent piece of acting, and now it was Bellos's turn to be useful.

Carlos checked his watch. 10.59 p.m. If Bellos didn't get here in the next minute or two, Carlos's plan would be completely derailed. Bellos had told him that the localised CCTV cameras would be disabled from 10.55 to 11.02 – that was the longest time period he could offer.

The seconds passed agonisingly fast as Carlos's anxiety levels reached new heights. But just as he was starting to really panic, Bellos appeared from a side door and, after taking a quick look over his shoulder, marched straight towards a large black gate.

Bellos reached the gate and swiped a card through a panel at its side. The door clicked and swung open. Bellos threw some sort of parcel through the gate and hurried back towards the building.

The second he was out of sight, Carlos sprang forward. The black door was time-coded to stay fully open for just ten seconds and then close quickly. It was about twenty metres away, and by the time Carlos was halfway across the courtyard, its ten seconds of opening time were over.

Frantically, Carlos rushed forwards, watching in horror as the door began to close. He sped on – the door had now reached the halfway point of closure. In another few seconds, his chance would be gone. As the gate reached the final quarter of closure, Carlos launched himself through the air, smashed against the door's surface and ricocheted past it and out onto a gravel concourse. He looked back and in horror saw that the door was about to close on his right foot and crush it to pulp. With a frantic tug he just managed to yank it free.

The door slammed shut behind him with a clang.

Sweating and pumped up with adrenalin, Carlos grabbed Bellos's parcel and opened it rapidly. It contained a set of clothes and a pair of brogues. If he stayed in his prison gear, he wouldn't get far. It took him thirty seconds to swap clothes. He stuffed his prison outfit into the bag and ran across the concourse. At the end he turned left onto a large and deserted street. For a second he gazed at a photo he'd lifted from the pocket of his prison shirt.

"Don't worry," he said to the photo in Spanish, "I won't let you down." He placed it in his new shirt, before breaking into a run and disappearing into the night.

CHAPTER 5
Season Set-up

When Nat walked into the kitchen the next morning, Inés was sitting at the table reading a newspaper.

"Are you happy with toast and jam and coffee for breakfast?" she asked, looking up. "We don't eat big breakfasts round here. If you want something more substantial, I can easily make it, though."

"Toast and coffee is perfect," replied Nat.

"You're not training at Talorca's La Plaza Stadium," Inés explained, standing up to put some bread in the toaster. "Talorca are taking turns with the teams in their group to train there. The teams in your group will be based at one of our neighbouring clubs, Sporting El Mar. *El mar* means 'the sea'."

Nat knew El Mar. They were in the Spanish second division and had just missed out on promotion last season.

"Their ground is inland," explained Inés. "Is it OK if we leave in fifteen minutes?"

"That's fine," nodded Nat.

"I'll be taking you to training every day," smiled Inés, "and I'll be around to chauffeur you other places if you need."

Nat, who loved his independence, baulked slightly at this. "You don't have to take me *everywhere*," he replied. "I'd like to catch a Spanish bus sometime and I'm sure I'll travel some places on the team coach."

"Whatever suits you," replied Inés.

Nat ate three pieces of toast spread with tasty peach jam and poured himself a cup of strong coffee.

"There's a piece about the tournament on the back pages of the paper," said Inés. "Would you like to see it?"

"Er . . . my Spanish is very basic," responded Nat. "I'd hardly be able to read a word."

"No problem," said Inés, taking the paper and scanning the story.

"Oh," she said after a minute.

"What is it?" asked Nat.

"It's . . . er . . . just something from Talorca's captain, Alberto Tieras. He loves the sound of his own voice. I'm sure you don't want to hear it."

"No, go on," said Nat.

"Alright," she sighed, "here goes. Tieras claims that Talorca should easily win their group and progress to Saturday's final. 'Marseilles and Hamburg should be no match for us, and we're confident of progressing,' he declared. Asked about the teams in the other group, Tieras paid a minimum of respect to Celtic and Lazio, but reserved some biting criticism for the late replacement, English team Hatton Rangers."

Inés looked up from the paper. "Are you sure you want me to go on?" she enquired.

"Absolutely!" nodded Nat.

"In Tieras's words, 'Hatton Rangers are a tiny outfit from the backwoods of English football. They've only just made it to the top level and spent a whole season facing the drop. We would have much preferred Everton to have been here because they are a big-name club. I mean, Hatton who?' said Tieras."

Inés grimaced and put the paper down. "I don't think a diplomatic career will beckon for Tieras after he's finished with football," she smiled apologetically, as if his words were her fault.

"Definitely not," agreed Nat, a bit shocked that the captain of the tournament's host team would be so liberal in spreading bile about Hatton Rangers before a ball had been kicked.

A few minutes later, Nat was inside Inés's red Fiat, on his way to training. They cut through olive groves and dusty hills, finally picking up a more substantial road until Inés pulled up in front of the El Mar Stadium. It was no La Plaza, but it was surrounded by four pretty chunky stands. Nat knew its capacity was 20,000. That was 10,000 less than Hatton Rangers's Ivy Stadium, but it still looked big. Its front facade was painted in El Mar's colours – purple and white.

As Nat climbed out of the Fiat and thanked Inés for the ride, the Hatton Rangers team bus came into view.

"I'll see you tonight," said Inés, giving him a wave and driving away.

The Rangers players started filing off the coach.

"Hey Nat!" called Adilson, Rangers's skilful Brazilian midfielder. "How's it going? Did you miss us?"

Nat laughed.

"Don't worry," grinned Adilson, "the boss had us going to bed early like good boys. But I bet him and Evans stayed down in the bar for a few drinks!"

A red sports car pulled up, driven by an older man with a grey ponytail and large sunglasses. Emi got out of the passenger side. "See you later, Pedro!" he called out, before the sports car sped off. Nat got on well with Emi – a six foot three nineteen year-old, who'd already made ten appearances for the Ivory Coast senior side. There was often a spark of mischief in his intense dark brown eyes.

"That guy is a serious dude!" laughed Emi, walking over to join Nat and Adilson. "He had me up 'til all hours showing me his poker tricks!"

Nat and Adilson laughed and they followed everyone else through the front door of the stadium, across a marble-tiled concourse, down some stairs, along a corridor that smelt of engine oil, and into a changing room.

It was nowhere near as smart and comfortable as their changing room back at the Ivy Stadium, but it was clean and functional. Stan Evans was placing training kit on the benches round the room. The club physiotherapist Colin Dempsey and publicity woman Helen Aldershot were the only other members of the Rangers staff accompanying Fox and Evans on the trip.

Nat found a space on the benches and started getting changed.

At that moment, the changing room door flew open and Kelvin burst in. "I am staying with a totally crazy family!" he groaned, making a beeline for Nat and Emi. Kelvin was short and muscular – a dead ringer for Brazilian legend Roberto Carlos. At twenty, he was firmly established as the England under-twenty-ones' right-back.

"Crazy in what way?" asked Emi.

"They have seven year-old twin boys, who got me to sign everything in their house. I mean EVERYTHING – tables, chairs, even their teddy bears!"

"It makes a change to be wanted!" shouted the Wildman.

The whole changing room, including Kelvin, erupted in laughter.

"Listen up!" declared Ian Fox, striding into the room. "This is where the serious business starts!"

Fox was hugely respected both within Hatton Rangers and by the outside world. He'd taken the club from the fourth tier right up to the Premier League in seven seasons, with a limited budget and a skeleton staff.

Nat did up his bootlaces and sat down with everyone else. He could feel the nerves jangling inside him. Here he was again with the real Hatton Rangers squad, about to start training. No matter how many times he'd sat with these players – who until a few months ago were his heroes on posters and in newspapers – it still felt totally surreal.

"Welcome back to the world of professional football!" boomed Fox.

Emi winked at Nat.

"It's good to see that everyone has reached this point without picking up any serious injuries – no tripping over kids' paddling pools, falling down stairs carrying their kids' computers or getting ruptured stomachs due to excessive ice cream consumption."

Everyone laughed. Robbie Clarke groaned. He was the one who'd broken his arm after falling downstairs – just before the Tottenham game at the end of the season. Luckily it hadn't been too bad a break and the club doctor had passed him as fit two weeks ago.

"So let's cut straight to the serious bit," continued Fox. "If there's anyone in this room who thinks this is some kind of jolly, they might as well get changed and make their way to the airport. This is where our new season begins and I am utterly determined to make sure that this season is very different from the last. Being so perilously close to relegation from the off was not good for the nerves or the heart."

"Too right!" agreed the Wildman.

"Your performance against Manchester United was the

best of the season. After all of my lectures and demands, you finally started playing like a team. And that's what I want you to do out here. The better you gel as a group over the course of this tournament, the better our chance of making a good start to the season back home."

There were nods all round the room.

"This is not some meaningless kick around in the sun. This is a tournament in which we will be competing alongside five world-class teams – teams who have all won numerous trophies. Our lack of silverware might make them think we're some lightweight outfit, here just to make up the numbers, but we're going to prove them wrong. We start the tournament on equal terms with those other teams. There'll be people back home and all over the world watching these games and we mustn't let ourselves down."

Nat swallowed nervously. *What happens if Lazio and Celtic completely smash us? It would be such a confidence destroyer before the start of the new Premier League season.*

"And there's another important aspect to this tournament," continued Fox. "Phone Valve – the company sponsoring this tournament – have made a commitment to pouring some sponsorship money into the winning team."

There were raised eyebrows all round the changing room.

"For the Talorcas and Lazios of this world, the sum we're talking about might be peanuts, but to us it would represent a fundamental financial leg-up, and take a bit of pressure off our chairman. As you know, Steve Pritchard has put millions into this club."

Nat knew – because Fox had told him and his father – that if Hatton Rangers had been relegated, Steve Pritchard would have bowed out of the club and bankruptcy would have been a certainty.

"It's high time Mr Pritchard got some value for money. The Phone Valve sponsorship opportunity provides an extra dimension to our need to shine on the field out here. Does everyone get that?"

"Yes boss," chorused the Rangers players.

"Good," said Fox, "now let's get out there!"

CHAPTER 6
An Edgy Start

As the players jogged out of the changing room into the brightness of the day, Nat instantly saw that the pitch was in good condition for a small club. The earth around the goalmouths was exposed but on a par with some pitches back home.

Unlike some other clubs that employed first team coaches, Fox and Evans carried out all training sessions themselves. They wanted to see every move, and shape the way the side played.

"OK," Fox called out. "We'll start with some warm-ups and then some gentle running – to ease you boys in."

Nat was delighted to begin in this calm fashion. Since that last game of the season, he'd made sure he stayed fit and as match-ready as possible. He'd gone on long runs in the fields and meadows surrounding the cottage in the first two weeks. He'd also spent hours practising his shooting and free kicks in the large field at the back of the cottage. He worked on his angles, and on the power of his shots and had experimented with hitting balls high and low, swerving and dipping. He knew that if he had any chance of really making a career out of this, he'd constantly need to put in large amounts of extra work, just like all of his favourite players did.

He'd bought some dumb-bells from a shop in Lowerbury to build his upper body strength. He'd done thousands of press-ups and sit-ups. And the previous week he'd been going to Shelton Park every day to work out in the excellent gym. He'd seen a couple of the players there – Dean Jobson and Andy Young – but most of the squad relished the chance to have a complete break from the everyday pressures of being a professional footballer.

However, in spite of all of the work and time Nat had committed, there were still nagging doubts in his mind about his body strength and his ability. It wasn't a level playing field. The other players were much older than him – some were nearly twenty years his senior. Their bodies were much more developed than his – he was still growing. He knew he could pass and shoot and head the ball, but had his appearances at the end of last season just been flukes? Or had he had an easy introduction to top-level matches because his legs were fresh, whereas everyone else had been exhausted after playing so many games?

Stop worrying about all that and concentrate!

After the warm-ups and gentle jogs, they did some more demanding runs and then some dribbling work with cones in different zones of the pitch. Nat felt himself getting into his stride. He always enjoyed working by himself on his fitness and skills, but it felt great to be back with the rest of the squad. It also felt liberating to be without bitter ex-Rangers striker Steve Townsend, who had felt so seriously threatened by Nat's arrival that he'd tried to end his career by a vicious tackle in training. Nat had seen a tiny piece in the papers a couple of weeks back, linking Townsend with a couple of teams in the third tier of English football.

They can have him!

"Alright, lads," called out Fox. "I want defenders and midfielders with me, strikers and keepers go with Stan."

"This way, lads!" shouted Evans, jogging to the goal at the other end of the pitch.

Nat strolled after him with the strikers Dennis Jensen, Robbie Clarke and Nicky Sinclair. With first team goalie Chris Webb in prison, awaiting trial for the match-fixing scandal, the battle to become first-choice keeper was between the reserve team keeper Graham Dalston, a twenty-four-year-old who'd made seven first team appearances, and Jack Bell, a nineteen-year-old who'd so far only made it as far as the reserves. Both had played for England at youth level but up to now had missed out on further involvement with the national set-up. Ian Fox was keeping his eye out on several available goalies from other clubs, but he'd told Dalston and Bell that if they worked hard and played well, a new keeper could end up as third choice behind them.

Ian Fox had bought Nicky Sinclair from Aberdeen as soon as the summer transfer window opened. With Steve Townsend gone, he had to invest in another forward. He'd got Sinclair for an undisclosed sum, which often meant very little. Sinclair was twenty-five and had become frustrated by being a perennial substitute at Aberdeen. Fox had promised him he'd get a decent slice of first team action, so he'd been happy to move south, even though it meant uprooting his wife and baby daughter.

Sinclair was six foot one and wiry, with a shock of ginger hair jutting out from his forehead. He was quiet and only really spoke if someone asked him a question. But he was agile, good in the air and a hard worker – the sort of player Ian Fox and Stan Evans liked. In the strikers' pecking order, Nat assumed that Robbie Clarke and Dennis Jensen were now first and second choice strikers, with him third and Nicky Sinclair fourth. But you never knew how the boss was thinking.

"Alright," said Evans, when he and the six players were standing by the goal. "Graham and Jack will face twelve shots each – you attackers will each take four shots at whoever's in goal. That means you'll all get to face both of them. Graham, you're first in."

Dalston walked into the goal, bent his knees and stretched his arms in readiness.

The strikers lined up at the edge of the penalty area, with Jensen first, next Clarke, then Nat, and finally Sinclair. Evans stood next to a huge net of balls, twenty yards to the right of the goal. He picked out a ball and lobbed it towards the penalty spot. Jensen hit it on the volley but Dalston tipped it over the bar. Evans whipped in another and Jensen skied it.

From then on, the balls flew into the area and when Jensen and Clarke had had their four shots, it was Nat's turn. He rubbed his hands together nervously as Evans lobbed a ball towards him. He let it bounce and caught it on the half volley. It hurtled towards the top left corner but Dalston dived and caught it. His second attempt was a cracking volley that hit the left post. He over-hit his third shot but his fourth, a curling volley, whistled into the back of the net. Dalston grimaced.

"Nice one, Nat!" shouted Evans encouragingly.

Nat was pleased he'd scored, but one out of four wasn't a great tally. For the next half hour, Nat and the strikers hit shot after shot at Dalston and Bell. Nat's average stayed at one in four, the same as Nicky Sinclair, while Jensen and Clarke averaged two. This strike rate bothered Nat and he felt a small wave of panic rising inside him. Dennis Jensen spotted his slightly crestfallen expression and said, "Don't be down on yourself, Nat. This is only our first session back. You're a great finisher."

Nat felt a bit patronised by this comment but he knew that Jensen was just trying to lift his spirits.

Half an hour later, Fox shouted over, "We're going to play some five-a-side now."

The strikers, goalies and Evans walked back down

the pitch to meet up with the others. Fox had a piece of paper in his hand. He showed it to Evans and they held a quick discussion.

"This is the first five-a-side team," announced Fox, putting Nat in a team with Jack Bell, Sinclair, Emi, and the Wildman. The team they were to play included Dalston, Kelvin and Adilson.

From the kick-off, Nat saw little of the ball. He finally exchanged several passes with Emi and had a decent, dipping shot saved by Dalston. But despite trying to forget the shooting practice earlier, his poor goal-to-strike ratio was still gnawing at him. What had happened to all of the striking practice he'd put in over the last couple of months? He tried to shake this out of his mind, but it rankled, and he missed a good chance provided by a cross from the Wildman, by stabbing it wide. He then went on a decent run, bypassing Adilson's attempt at a tackle, but was blocked by Kelvin. The next few minutes saw the opposing team attacking – a period which culminated in Adilson scoring with a wickedly curling shot. Nat had another chance a minute later, but it sailed just over the crossbar.

When Fox called time, Nat was disappointed with his performance. This wasn't the way he'd envisaged his first training session back with the team.

Think about what Jensen said. Give yourself a break!

Another two teams fought out a one-one draw, and then Nat's team were selected to play a team consisting of Graham Dalston, Andy Young, Pierre Sacrois, Paulo Carigio and Jermaine Clifton. Nat started this game well and linked up with Sinclair to strike a volley at Dalston, which the keeper saved. Pierre Sacrois, the right-sided, French midfielder, was on fire and twice he outwitted Emi and the Wildman to grab half-chances, the second of which he smashed into the back of Bell's net. Nat groaned.

I have to up my game here or I'll have no chance of playing in this tournament at all!

A minute later, Emi lofted a ball over Andy Young's head. Nat ran on to it, controlled it on his knee and hit a low volley. The ball flew at great speed, but it was too near to Graham Dalston and Dalston managed to catch it. Nat sprinted forward, hoping Dalston might spill the ball, but he held on to it tightly. Another shot – another missed opportunity.

As Dalston rolled out the ball to Paulo Carigio, something caught Nat's eye and his gaze drifted away from the pitch. In the stand nearest to where the action was taking place stood a lone figure, bathed in shadow. It was a rather spindly man, wearing a navy blue suit. He had short grey hair and held a briefcase in his left hand. Nat caught his eye. The man seemed to be watching him.

Nat couldn't see his features very well, but a feeling of unease suddenly seeped inside him. Could this guy be somehow connected to the match-fixing plot and Nat's role in stopping it? Was he tied in some way to Chris Webb and his thuggish co-plotter Tanner? Nat was pretty sure he'd cost someone hundreds of thousands, if not millions of pounds. Nat's story had featured in the *Sunday Crest* as an exclusive, but all of the other papers had given it plenty of coverage too. What if this guy was out here in Spain to exact some kind of revenge on Nat? It was a horrible thought.

"NAT!" shouted a voice, dragging his brain from these thoughts. Emi had just played a ball to Nat at head height, but he was too late in reacting, and Pierre Sacrois out-jumped him, heading the ball to Jermaine Clifton, who ran on and fired it past a diving Jack Bell.

The Wildman shook his head and motioned that he wanted to restart the game as quickly as possible, to level the score.

"Come on, Nat!" shouted the Wildman. "Let's get back in this!"

"Definitely!" nodded Nat.

In spite of the sun's powerful rays, he shivered and quickly stole a glance back at the stand. But now there was nothing to see.

The man had gone.

CHAPTER 7
Poolside Chill

Nat only touched the ball once more in the mini game and that was for a pass that went out. Another two teams played a final five-a-side game and then training was over. The players filed back towards the changing room while Stan Evans went round the pitch collecting all of the balls in a large net. Ian Fox, who was standing by the touchline, beckoned for Nat to come over to him. The Rangers manager waited until everyone else had left the pitch before he spoke.

"What's up?" he asked.

Nat frowned.

"You seemed to be somewhere else for those five-a-sides," observed Fox. "Is there something you need to tell me?"

Nat's eyes quickly scanned the stand again. It was still empty. Should he tell Fox about the man and his suspicions? Should he explain his fear of reprisal? Or was he being ridiculous? On balance, it was probably better to leave it. He didn't want Fox thinking he'd become

paranoid over the summer and sending him home. He also
didn't want the Rangers boss getting the Spanish police
involved if the man turned out to be just a groundsman
or something.

"I'm fine," replied Nat.

"You didn't look fine. You were all over the place. Your
passes were off. Your shooting was poor."

"I wasn't *that* bad," replied Nat, his cheeks burning. He
immediately regretted the defiance of his tone.

"Look, Nat," said Fox, lowering his voice. "I know
you're here in completely different circumstances from
everyone else. I know you're only thirteen and that this
whole assumed identity business is still mind-blowing for
you. But we agreed at the outset that if things ever got out
of hand you'd report to me, and that if your performances
weren't up to scratch I'd report to you."

"I know, boss," replied Nat in a much calmer voice. "I'm
sorry. Things haven't got out of hand. It's just getting back
into the swing of things. I didn't quite get there today. But
I'll be totally different in training tomorrow. I promise."

"I'm not being harsh, but there's very little margin for
error out here," added Fox. "We have two, possibly three,
games in the space of a week and if you don't catch up
with the others, you won't be seeing any action. You have
to understand that."

"I do," replied Nat, trying to hide the anger he
was feeling.

I saved this club from relegation and bankruptcy and

Fox is down on me like a mountain of bricks because of one training session!

"Good," nodded Fox. "Now go and get changed and then come back to the hotel and relax with everyone else. We'll see tomorrow's training session as a fresh start, OK?"

Back in the changing room, Nat spoke to no one. His heart felt heavy after Fox's comments. What happened if he didn't improve his game tomorrow? After his end-of-season highs, it would be so crushing to play no part in this tournament. He waited his turn to get into the showers, had a thorough soak and got changed.

The players were just about to move out of the changing room when there was some noise near the door and in walked a round-bellied man, with a smooth scalp and a thin moustache. His suit was charcoal grey and immaculately tailored. A crisp white handkerchief jutted out of the right pocket of his jacket. He was flanked by two burly men in less immaculate suits, who seemed closer to the ape species than the human one. Another man in jeans and a t-shirt was taking photos of him with an expensive-looking camera.

"Mr Mabena!" beamed Ian Fox, walking over to give the man a hearty handshake. The photographer snapped the two men shaking hands.

"Mr Fox! It has been a while since we last met. I believe it was during a Talorca v Arsenal game eleven years ago?"

The photographer snapped again.

"That's right," smiled Fox, turning to address his players. "Gentlemen, this is Victor Mabena – the President of Talorca FC. I've known him for over twenty years. He pretty much built the club up from nothing by himself and he's the mover behind this tournament."

The photographer took another few shots.

"You are very kind, Mr Fox," smiled Mabena with an appreciative nod. "I have very great respect for English football and follow your Premier League closely, so it is an honour to have you here."

"Thank you," said Fox on behalf of the team.

"I have been visiting all the tournament teams," went on Mabena, "and I am very much looking forward to the opening games this evening. My aim is to ensure that each and every one of you has a positive experience with us. If there is anything you need, please do not hesitate to ask a member of the Talorca staff and feel free to ask for me personally, should the need arise."

"A Learjet would be nice," whispered Kelvin. Nat had to smother a laugh.

The photographer clicked his camera several more times.

"I will of course be at the Talorca games when you play the games against Celtic and Lazio in your mini-league, but if you make it through to the final I will see you all at La Plaza Stadium, regardless of whether Talorca make it through or not."

Mabena then shook Fox's hand again, posed for

some more photos and swept out of the room, his two henchmen and his photographer at his side.

"Come on, lads!" declared Stan Evans a minute after Mabena had gone. "Let's head for the bus and get some downtime."

As Nat walked towards the team bus his mobile went.

"Dad?"

"Hey Nat, how was training?"

Nat edged away from his teammates and spoke in a low whisper.

"It wasn't great."

"Why not?"

Nat thought about mentioning the man in the stands but again thought better of it. Why freak his dad out when he knew nothing about the guy and might be being ridiculous?

"I was just a bit off the pace."

"Surely most people were?"

"Yeah, I suppose so. Anyway I'm just about to get on the team bus. I'll give you a bell later or tomorrow."

"Are you alright?"

"I'm fine, but I've got to go."

"OK, but don't worry too much about training, you've only just got there."

The call ended and Nat stepped onto the coach, thinking about his tête-à-tête with Fox. He was put out by the manager's words, but having gone over them several times in his head, he had to reluctantly admit that they were true – he *had* lost concentration during training. It was all connected to the man in the stands. While deciding to keep an eye out for the man, Nat also resolved to act on Fox's promise that the following day's training would represent a new start. He would give absolutely everything tomorrow and try and forget about the man – who would probably turn out to be no one important, anyway.

Spirits on the bus were high. Adilson sung a Portuguese song very badly, but gained a massive cheer for his efforts. The driver then flicked on the radio and blasted several 'golden oldies' out of the speakers, which the older players joined in with, while Nat, Emi, Kelvin and the other younger players shouted at them for being 'past it'.

When the bus arrived at the hotel, Nat's own spirits rose. It was a large white building, with several brown and gold domes, reflecting the Moorish influences in Andalusia. Its lobby was cavernous, with a huge chrome reception desk taking up almost the entire left side of the space. Large round glass windows in the ceiling made it extremely light.

"This is definitely more chilled out than where I'm staying!" laughed Kelvin.

Outside, guests were dotted round the edges of the pool, lying on sunloungers, soaking up rays, reading books or snoozing.

"Top class!" grinned Emi.

Nat, Emi and Kelvin strolled to some loungers and flopped down onto them. A minute later, a waiter approached and asked if they'd like anything to drink. They all ordered cokes.

After twenty minutes of chatting, Nat and Emi went to get changed into their trunks and hit the pool. Nat had been to plenty of swimming pools around the world but none of them had been this luxurious. An intricate pattern of light blue tiles covered the pool floor, the water shimmered in the sunshine.

After an hour in the pool, Nat dried off and sat for a while on his lounger, reading a John Grisham novel. He loved thrillers – the plot twists, the action scenes, the biting dialogue – and always got drawn into the worlds where the action took place.

After a while Kelvin announced, "It's table tennis time!"

The table tennis table was situated outside, under a huge awning so it was shady. Kelvin was a decent player but Nat was his equal. After an hour, Nat was four games to three up and they called it a day.

It was close to six o'clock when Stan Evans came round announcing it was time to eat, after which the team bus would be taking them all to watch the opening match in their group – Celtic v Lazio – back at the El Mar Stadium.

The hotel dining room was empty, as the majority of guests were Spanish and would therefore be eating supper much later. The meal consisted of *gazpacho Andaluz*, a cold tomato soup with garlic, peppers and olive oil, followed by generous helpings of fish and chicken, accompanied by spinach and chickpea salad and baby asparagus stewed with onions, coriander and lemon juice. It was all excellent and Nat washed his food down with a large glass of still lemonade that was tasty, but nowhere near as good as Inés's. With such delights on offer, some of the players – particularly Dean Jobson – slightly overdid it, a fact that gained a disapproving look from Ian Fox, who'd had to talk to Jobson about his post-summer-holiday weight a couple of times in the past.

When they'd eaten their fill, the players were served portions of thin apple cake and bowls of dried fruit and nuts.

"I'm stuffed," said Nat, patting his stomach.

"Me too!" agreed Emi. "It's a good thing we haven't got a game tonight!"

On the team bus, Nat played cards with Emi, Kelvin and Adilson and felt very relaxed. The afternoon of leisure had been good for him after the intensity of training and the anxiety relating to the man in the stands. After all, he told himself, he was in Spain with the Hatton Rangers first team squad – it was an experience to relish.

CHAPTER 8
Hunted

Carlos shivered, desperate for it to get dark. The sunlight was fading but the last rays seemed to be stubbornly battling to stay in the sky. He'd spent hours lying in this ditch in soaking wet clothes, checking his watch every few minutes. As soon as it was fully dark, he would emerge and find a phone. He'd had the mobile Bellos gave him in his prison trousers, but it had fallen out some time during the previous night. Going back to look for it was an impossibility. He had to stay completely out of sight. If anyone saw him and reported him to the police, he'd be back in prison like a thunderbolt. The lost phone had been pay-as-you-go and he was certain it wouldn't be traceable back to Bellos.

He had to phone Rudy as soon as possible. They were on an extremely tight schedule and any unnecessary waiting would leave them without time to complete the task they had set themselves. He knew Rudy would come and get him, it was just a question of when he'd be able to make a call. Carlos thought back for the hundredth time about the drama of the night before.

A feeling of elation had coursed through his veins in the minutes after he'd escaped from the prison, but he was well aware that his disappearance would be discovered very soon. He'd only been running for a few minutes when he heard the screech of sirens and saw the frantic flash of blue and red lights behind him. Sprinting to the end of the main street, he'd vaulted over a small wall and down onto a path running alongside a river.

The sirens and lights had quickly moved in and he heard voices in the street above. A minute later, a torch beam shone down onto the river and the bank. In panic, Carlos had silently lowered himself in, the chilly water seeping into his bones. So much for the fresh set of clothes Bellos had provided for him. He'd held his breath for as long as he could and then surfaced. To his horror, a policeman had jumped over the wall and was now walking at the side of the river, throwing large arcs of yellow light across the water with his torch.

Carlos's heart sank. Was this going to be it? Would he be discovered less than ten minutes after his break-out? He'd be the laughing stock, not just in his prison, but in every police station throughout the country.

Knowing he had to put space between himself and the policeman on the bank, he started swimming underwater. He swam as far as he could before he needed to take in some air. Thankfully he was a strong swimmer.

He went underwater again, but this time when he rose, he saw to his horror that the police officer had been joined by a colleague and they were striding up the bank in his direction.

Feeling panic grip him, Carlos increased his pace, using strong arm and leg strokes, while making minimal noise. Up the river he swam, but every time he looked back, it seemed that the officers were getting nearer. After another minute of swimming, Carlos made a snap decision – if he stayed in the water he was bound to be found sooner or later. So as quickly as he could, he swam to the opposite bank and, with stiff arms, pulled himself out of the water.

"Hey! What was that?" yelled the first officer, shining his torch across at the opposite bank. The beam missed Carlos's right foot by a couple of millimetres. Carlos almost yelped in desperation and flung himself into a large bush beside the bank.

"Did you hear something?" shouted the first officer.

"No," replied his colleague.

"I swear I heard something!"

"There's a bridge up ahead. Let's go check it out."

Carlos didn't need any further warning. He fought his way through the dense bush and emerged on the other side by a stone archway. He hurried through it and found himself on a building site. It was a half-built new development with several apartments and the outline of a large car park. In his cold, exhausted state he was tempted to run inside the section that was finished and at least spend the night there, but he rejected this option quickly. Firstly, it was far too near the prison and secondly, he'd probably be discovered by builders turning up early the next morning. No, he needed to strike out much further.

So, with shaking bones, he skirted round the development and picked up a decent stride, running for several miles at the edge of a narrow road, through hedges until he finally stopped at 4.30 a.m., dog-tired, wet and terribly cold. When he'd seen the ditch, he'd pretty much fallen headfirst into it, sleeping fitfully until the first rays of morning sunlight prodded him awake.

On waking, he discovered that the ditch was near a small village. Over the next twelve hours he'd only seen five people pass and no one had come anywhere near his hiding place. But he hadn't dared to emerge in the light, even though he was desperate to locate a phone booth.

Carlos shivered again and his mind snapped out of last night's escape and jumped back to the present. The sun continued on its agonisingly slow downward movement and, at that moment, he heard a snuffling sound in the distance. He raised his head a couple of centimetres and saw an elderly man walking a small but vicious-looking, brown, slavering dog. Carlos gulped and lowered himself back down, hoping the two of them would just pass.

But in mounting fear, he listened as their footsteps got closer and the dog started making yowling sounds. The man shouted something at him. The dog's snarling suddenly got much louder and Carlos heard its feet trying to drag the man in the direction of the ditch. Carlos considered running down the ditch to avoid possible discovery, but this would make noise and would alert the dog even further to his presence. He stayed put and closed his eyes, willing them to leave.

The dog was now barking ferociously and Carlos heard the two of them almost upon him. He'd be spotted any second now. His whole body tensed, ready to spring when they looked down at him. If he attacked the man, the dog would probably go crazy. It was probably better to attack the dog, or to just run. But the man snapped loudly and gave the chain a mighty yank. The dog growled bitterly but the man was resolute and dragged his pet with scraping footsteps away from the ditch.

Three minutes later, their progress was almost out of earshot. Carlos wiped his clammy hands on the back of his damp shirt. That had been an incredibly close shave. What if the man and his dog returned shortly and this time the man let the dog off the leash? It wasn't dark yet, but Carlos felt he had no choice but to move. He waited another ten minutes, then pulled himself out of the ditch.

He checked there was no one else around and ran as fast as he could towards the village, praying he'd find a phone box.

CHAPTER 9
Fierce Opponents

Nat was excited about watching the Celtic v Lazio game live. He'd seen Lazio on TV a few times in the previous season and they were a strong outfit with several excellent players. Among their ranks was one genuinely world-class footballer – the home-grown playmaker Arturo Tassi. At eighteen years old, he'd already played for the senior Italian side and was talked of as the new 'Zidane' by the Italian press. Mind you, lots of players had been called the new Zidane over the years, and none of them had ever lived up to the name.

For Nat, Zidane or 'Zizou' as his teammates had called him, was the greatest player of all time. Nat had lost track of how many times he'd watched clips on the internet of Zidane in his prime. What astonished Nat was the man's ability to receive and control the ball from any height or angle, and in the same move to take it past an opposing player. It was utterly incredible to watch and very, very difficult to copy. Zidane's balance was remarkable and his skilful legs and feet had bamboozled countless defenders over the years.

Marking Zidane or trying to wrest the ball off him looked like a thankless task – the man had kept possession like no one else. And if that wasn't enough, his passing was exemplary and his finishing sublime. He really possessed it all. It didn't matter to Nat that Zidane had bowed out of the game with his infamous head-to-chest butt in the 2006 World Cup Final against Italy. He was a complete legend and nothing would change Nat's desire to emulate the great man in whatever way he could.

As well as Tassi, Lazio had Luigi Fellini, a bulky centre-forward, who was fearless and very strong and didn't mind getting stuck in. Their incredibly fast left-back, Roger Salba from Cameroon, scored far more goals than almost every other player who played in his position. But Nat had seen Lazio lose games to 'lesser' opposition in the last twelve months. In spite of the first team costing about £200 million, he got the feeling that some of their players were resting on their reputations and not giving it their all. This was a weakness and Nat hoped that Hatton Rangers would be able to exploit it when they came up against the Italians.

The Celtic team cost a fraction of that and their manager Roddy Hanwell was well-known for developing Scottish talent. They'd only just missed out on winning the Scottish Premier League last season and had made it to the quarter finals of the Champions League, so they weren't a side to be sniffed at.

The latest player to come through their youth ranks

was a central midfielder called Gavin Clyde. He was a tall lad, and when you first saw him you thought he'd be awkward and ungainly. But the opposite was true. He moved quickly and gracefully with excellent ball control. His passing was superb and he could split a defence with his vision. He also scored goals and linked up particularly well with the Celtic forwards Jimmy Doode and the stocky Bulgarian Ilio Camporda. If the Lazio players thought they'd trample on Celtic, they'd badly underestimated them.

The El Mar Stadium had been totally transformed from the quiet place of this morning's training session. Spectators were streaming in through the turnstiles, many of them wearing Spain shirts, although Nat also spotted a decent-sized bunch of both Lazio and Celtic fans in their club's colours, all mingling with each other and sharing plenty of good-natured banter.

The Hatton Rangers players were led through a side entrance and down a maze of corridors until they reached the stands. The stadium's floodlights threw huge white beams across the turf. Stan Evans led the players up an aisle and ushered them to their seats. They were sitting in some of the best in the stadium – on the halfway line five rows back, just behind the Lazio and Celtic benches. A tournament programme was passed around. It was in Spanish and, because of their very late withdrawal, Everton were the English team listed and the profiles and photos were of their players.

"Look out for Tassi," Nat said to Emi.

"I will do," nodded Emi. "I saw him when Lazio played Juventus in March and he was on fire – scored this outrageous goal from outside the penalty area."

"I saw it," replied Nat. "And he's fast too."

"You wait," chipped in Kelvin. "Angus Reakin will nobble him."

Reakin was the Celtic captain – a brute of a man, who was known for his steely determination and bravery (some would say recklessness) in the tackle. For a man who scythed so many strikers, it was remarkable how few times he'd been sent off in his career.

When the two teams emerged from the tunnel they were greeted by a very warm reception – Celtic in their home kit of horizontal green and white striped shirts, white shorts and hooped green and white socks, Lazio in one of their away kits of yellow shirts, black shorts and yellow and black striped socks.

The Swedish referee called Angus Reakin and the Lazio captain Ade Ragani to the centre circle and tossed a coin. Celtic won the toss and Reakin opted for kick off. The referee checked with his assistants that they were ready and in place, and then blew his whistle for kick off.

The match started at a furious pace. The Celtic number five, central-defender Paul Smithfield, went flying into a couple of strong tackles on Tassi. But the young Italian seemed completely unfazed by these challenges and, more importantly for Lazio, didn't pick up any serious knocks.

The referee gave Smithfield a stern lecture but didn't resort to a yellow card. Reakin was Smithfield's partner in central defence and Nat saw that both of them were surprisingly quick for big players. He felt a shiver of anxiety. If he managed to significantly improve his game in training tomorrow and Fox gave him a bit of a run out in Tuesday night's match against Celtic, he'd be up against these two giants – a terrifying prospect.

Lazio attacked strongly in the first fifteen minutes, but Reakin and Smithfield were up to their advances. They out-jumped the Lazio players on corners and free kicks, and with the help of their teammates, denied Tassi any clear shooting opportunities. The Italian, seeing his path being continually blocked, changed tack and started hanging back, picking the ball up deeper and running at the Celtic players. On one incredible run, he rounded four Celtic players before squaring the ball to French striker Laurent Breton, whose thunderous shot bounced off the crossbar.

This gave Lazio encouragement to mount another couple of Tassi-inspired attacks. But a goal eluded them. And a few minutes later, after another attack, Celtic hit them on the break.

Smithfield took the ball out of the penalty area and hit it to left midfielder Nigel Flort. Flort was fast and skinned the Lazio right-back Franco Dessoti. He skipped over another challenge, took the ball into the penalty area and flicked it to Gavin Clyde, who hammered it home.

The Celtic players mobbed Clyde and Flort and their fans went ballistic, cheering and yelling and singing and waving their green and white scarves.

A shocked Lazio came back at them and had several good chances to equalise but couldn't get the ball in the back of the Celtic net. With the score still at one-nil to Celtic, the whistle went for half-time.

In the break, the Rangers Players were handed tea, coffee and slices of lemon cake by several of the El Mar stewards.

"I could get used to this!" laughed the Wildman.

Stan Evans came over to chat to Nat, Emi and Kelvin. "Lazio won't take that score lying down," he mused. "They'll give Tassi a totally free role in the second half, just you watch him. It will be attack city."

"But then Celtic will hit them on the break again," countered Kelvin.

"Maybe," replied Evans, "but I think once Lazio score, Celtic will fade."

And as soon as the second half began, it was clear that Stan Evans, a keen student of team formations, was right. Arturo Tassi seemed to be everywhere. This totally confused the Celtic defence and made them edgy. Sometimes he'd take a corner, sometimes he'd hang back at free kicks. The Celtic players weren't sure if they should man-mark him, put two players onto him or just defend quite high up, in the hope that he wouldn't be able to break through.

But on seventy-seven minutes, after Lazio had launched a series of increasingly desperate attacks, the ball was thumped to Tassi on the right flank. He was challenged by Celtic left-back Rob Storey, but brushed him off. He sold Paul Smithfield a dummy and sprinted towards the box, where Angus Reakin was waiting for him. With an incredible series of mesmerising step-overs, Tassi took the ball past Reakin and fired a dipping shot into the top left-hand corner of Celtic's goal.

Celtic one – Lazio one.

Tassi disappeared under a pile of his ecstatic teammates.

Bruce Collins, the Celtic keeper, was incensed by his defenders and screamed at them for not stopping Tassi. "There were three of you on to him!" he hollered.

The Celtic defenders glared furiously at their goalie, their stares shouting, *"You* were the one who didn't stop the shot going in."

Collins sulkily picked the ball out of the net and hoofed it towards the centre circle. The next ten minutes were pretty rough and tumble, with both teams dishing out over-the-top challenges, earning yellow cards for Angus Reakin and Paul Smithfield for Celtic, and Ade Ragani for Lazio.

In the last few minutes, Lazio had a chance to win the match when Laurent Breton hit the outside of the right post and then, at the other end, Lazio's goalie, Paulo Calari pulled off a magnificent reflex save with his legs from a fierce Gavin Clyde volley.

The final whistle went with the score fixed at one-one. The Celtic and Lazio players shook hands and exchanged shirts, before going to their respective fans and holding their arms aloft to clap them. Both sets of spectators seemed happy with the result.

"At least we know a bit more about both sides we'll be facing," said Stan Evans, as the Rangers party walked back through the corridors to the exit.

When they reached the front of the stadium Nat spotted Inés in her red Fiat a bit further down the road.

"I'll see you later," he said to Emi and Kelvin, before letting Fox and Evans know he was leaving.

"Did you get good seats?" asked Nat.

"Very good," replied Inés, "but I came by myself – José had other plans."

"A fair result?" asked Nat.

"Yes," nodded Inés, "I think so. Arturo Tassi is a big talent, isn't he?"

"Definitely. I thought he'd score at least one."

"I can't believe he's only eighteen," mused Inés. "He has a very bright future. Anyway, tell me about the rest of your day."

When Nat stopped talking and Inés had asked him lots of further questions, really showing an interest his answers, he couldn't help but think of his mum. Would talking to her have been like this? Would she have asked him the same kind of questions? Would she have known as much about football as Inés did?

That was one of the worst things about her dying when he was just six years old. There were so many questions he wanted to ask her, but he'd never get the chance. It was such a cruel blow.

He sighed and he and Inés lapsed into silence as they drove through the warm Andalusian night. It wasn't long before the jeep was heading down the path to the villa.

"Do you want something to eat?" asked Inés when they were inside.

"No thanks, I'm fine," replied Nat.

He went to his room and listened to his iPod for a while, before deciding to take a shower. He went to the bathroom but couldn't see any towels. He considered waiting until the morning, but then saw light spilling out from underneath Inés's door, so he knocked on it gently.

There was no reply, so he knocked again a bit louder. He eased the door open a fraction and saw that indeed the room was empty. And luckily there was a pile of towels stacked up on top of the dresser. He was just moving over to them, when he spotted a photo on the window ledge. It showed José looking quite a bit younger, Inés, and a man with medium length grey hair and piercing royal blue eyes.

"That is my husband – he was Italian."

Nat span round. Inés was standing in the doorway

looking at him. He quickly replaced the photo and pointed to the dresser.

"I c . . . c . . . came in here looking for a towel," he spluttered.

"No problem," she replied. "His name was Frederico – he died just over a year ago in a crash. Hardly a minute goes by when I don't think about him."

Nat remembered the smashed up motorbike in the wooden shed. No wonder it was in such a state; it had been involved in a fatal accident.

"I'm sorry," Nat said quietly. "I didn't know."

"Nor should you have," Inés smiled wistfully. "I didn't want to burden you on your trip. And anyway, José and I are surviving together. We're like an organism that's been smashed and is making every effort to reform, albeit in a different shape."

"It must be so hard," said Nat, biting his bottom lip, unsure whether he should tell her about his mother.

Inés sighed deeply. "It *is* very hard," she replied, "but I have my students and I have my home to look after. With the small pension my husband left me and my income from teaching, we have just enough to get by. José is looking for a job at the minute and when he gets one he'll insist on paying me rent. I miss my husband very much. I'm still grieving, but I'm going forwards – a little step each day."

They were silent for a few moments.

Shall I tell her?

Nat decided not to say anything. He edged past the bed and Inés stood aside to let him through.

"Good night Nat," she smiled. "I'll see you in the morning."

Nat went to take shower. It was just past midnight when he made it back to his room. He lay on the bed for a while, thinking. His mum had been killed by a car; Inés's husband – José's dad – had been killed in a motorbike crash. What a terrible way to lose your life. He shook these bleak thoughts from his mind and returned to his thriller novel.

Twenty minutes later, as he drifted off to sleep, he briefly thought about the next day. He'd need to be on top form in training. He had to prove himself to Ian Fox all over again.

CHAPTER 10
Back in Business

The same thoughts were the first thing that hit Nat when he woke up the next morning. He heard Ian Fox's words in his head, *If you don't catch up with the others, you won't be seeing any action.*

He checked his watch – 6.12 a.m. He got out of bed, threw on a t-shirt, shorts and trainers, grabbed his battered yellow and green football and crept down the corridor. Inés and José's doors were both closed. He took a pear from the fruit bowl on the kitchen table and left a short note telling Inés he'd gone out for a run.

The sun was already blazing when he left the villa, and the dry earth all around him looked more scorched than ever. He walked up the lane, down the hill and jogged all the way to the main road, by which time he was already drenched in sweat. He crossed the main road and carried on straight ahead, following a twisting track that passed a large field smelling of rosemary and contained a series of ash and willow trees.

And then he reached the sea. This part of the coastline

was miles from the tourist hot spots and it was very early in the morning, so he had the place to himself. Some rock pools were set among a collection of stones to his left. The sand was golden, soft and not too deep – a great condition for honing football skills.

Nat had decided that nerves had played a large part of his disappointing performance in training the day before – that and spotting the man in the stand. Well, that was dust now. Today, he'd be focusing totally on the session. If the guy appeared again, he'd deal with it, but he wasn't going to spend any time looking for him. Coming down here would push him that little bit further to be in shape for today's challenges.

He threw the ball skywards and trapped it with the underside of his right trainer. He then lifted it into the air and caught it on top of his head. Like a circus seal, he kept the ball there, only moving slightly on the balls of his heels. He then flicked it up and spent ten minutes keeping it in the air solely with his left foot and knee. Being right-footed, his left leg was obviously weaker, but he was always building it up and his left foot shot was closing the gap on his right one, both for power and placement.

He then placed the ball at his feet and sprinted along the sand, keeping it close to him, using both feet and making sharp swerves left and right. Nat always found it bizarre when football pundits praised a midfielder or an attacker, even though they couldn't 'beat a man'. What on earth did they mean? Surely apart from passing and tackling, the core skill of football was taking the ball past one or more opposing players. That's what gave your team the advantage and the momentum to have a crack at goal.

Up and down the beach Nat ran, imagining swathes of opposing defenders lunging at him to grab the ball but failing miserably. He was Zidane, gliding past a thicket of defenders. He was too fast and skilful for them, dragging the ball from their clutches, leaving them in his wake. As he ran, he thought of the year he'd lived in Rio de Janeiro with his dad. He'd spent vast stretches of time on the beach with the local kids and adults, watching, copying their multiple boxes of tricks. Nat had played and watched football in loads of countries but in Brazil it was different.

Football wasn't just a passion for Brazilians, it was in their lifeblood, it was part of their national DNA. And if he could keep working on some of the skills he'd picked up in Rio, then he'd be delivering something that few European players could offer.

After an hour of non-stop running, turning and kicking, he sat down on the sand and took a long drink from the bottle of water he'd brought with him. He closed his eyes and let the warmth of the sun wash over his body. He thought about the Celtic game tomorrow night. He *had* to play himself into the manager's reckoning. Surely three substitute appearances in the Premier League had shown Fox that he could handle himself against serious opposition? And he'd scored the winner against Manchester United. He couldn't go from that to missing out on a subs berth altogether. But the manager was very difficult to read. He was generally fair but sometimes he threw curveballs that took Nat completely by surprise.

Nat considered the Celtic defence. You had to respect their back four, especially the centre-backs, Reakin and Smithfield. They'd played pretty commandingly against Lazio and as long term teammates and defensive partners they knew each other's games extremely well. They were experts at keeping strikers out of their penalty area, forcing people to shoot from distance. They were very physical players who were more than happy to mix it up, bully attackers and play psychological games with them.

The left-back Rob Storey was a decent player too, but Davey Cathcart at right-back was a potential weak link. He had a much smaller frame than the other three, which gave him enormous stamina but laid him open to being pushed about by strikers. Plus he was a very attack-minded player, who often took the ball deep into the opposition half, leaving a gap behind him. Nat had seen him being exposed by forwards on a couple of occasions. It was definitely something to consider.

Nat stood up, wiped the sweat from his forehead and thumped the ball high in the air. He started running and when it crashed down, trapped it with the inside of his left boot, flicked it to his right foot and raced on. He repeated this procedure fifty times. When he looked at his watch again it was just coming up to 8.40 a.m. He'd done two hours of extra training. He could feel the effects of his hard work on his calf and back muscles but this was a feeling he welcomed. It showed he'd pushed himself a bit. Hopefully in training later he'd prove to the gaffer that he was serious about this tournament and wasn't prepared to miss out on the action.

When Nat returned, he found José out in the courtyard, just finishing up a call on his mobile. He put the phone in his pocket and raised his hand a few centimetres as a greeting. "You look like you've just run a marathon," José observed.

"I went down to the beach for some extra training," explained Nat, sitting down on the bench.

"That's good commitment," nodded José. "It shows you care. A lot of modern footballers only have their hearts on fast cars and nightclubs."

"No one at Hatton Rangers is really like that," replied Nat. "We did have a striker called Steve Townsend who was a massive gambler, but the manager kicked him out."

José sat down on the bench. "Football can be a glorious game," he murmured, "so long as people with the right spirit run it."

"Our manager's OK," mused Nat. "He's not world-famous or anything but he likes to get things done properly."

"Good managers do that," replied José with a slight smile, the first time Nat had seen any sort of positive expression on his face.

"We had a visit from Victor Mabena after training yesterday," said Nat.

José's smile instantly vanished and he leaned towards Nat. "Now that is someone who does *not* do things in the right spirit," he said, almost spitting out the words.

"What do you mean?" asked Nat.

"Mabena puts on the air of someone who is President because he's in love with the beautiful game, but people count for very little in Mabena's world. He loves the trappings of wealth – he's the worst type of person to be involved with a football club. The man's a snake!"

Nat was shocked by the ferocity of José's attack on the Talorca president, the flash-suited, beaming man he'd met yesterday at the El Mar Stadium. José clearly detested him.

"His great rival Huerto Figes nearly beat him to the presidency last year," added José. "There was talk of Mabena cheating but nothing was ever proved. The two of them hate each other."

Nat wasn't surprised by this. He'd heard of several bitter boardroom battles that had taken place at English clubs over the last few years.

"Your mum said you're looking for a job," said Nat, steering the discussion away from the Talorca President.

José shrugged his shoulders. "I'm out there all the

time," he responded with an underlying bitterness in his voice. "But work is scarce. Some people have said I should go further afield to look for a job, but why? This is my home."

"Gentlemen!" called Inés from the kitchen, breaking up the conversation. "Come and get something to eat."

The kitchen table had plates of toast, bowls of different jams, fruit, mugs, a pot of coffee and a milk jug.

Nat tucked into some toast and apricot jam. He was hungry after his workout. Inés bit into an apple while José poured himself some coffee and picked at a piece of toast.

After a few minutes of silent eating and drinking, José turned to his mother. "Victor Mabena went to see Nat and the rest of the Rangers players yesterday," he declared, with a contemptuous look on his face.

Inés said nothing.

"He makes it look like he's some honest, hard-working football fan," José went on. "But football is the last thing on his mind. The man has poisoned Talorca FC. He's filth!"

"OK, José, that's enough," said his mother sharply.

José went red in the face and snapped at her in Spanish. She snapped back. José then threw down his napkin and stormed out of the kitchen.

Nat sat in stunned silence for a few seconds. He looked to Inés for an explanation of this sudden eruption, but she looked away and poured herself another coffee.

After breakfast, Inés drove Nat to the El Mar Stadium. They talked about the Celtic v Lazio match and the weather. Inés's angry exchange with José wasn't mentioned.

Nat found everyone already in the same changing room they'd used yesterday. There was a lot of chat and teasing, particularly over the quality of Adilson's singing voice. He pretended to be offended but laughed with everyone else.

"All set for today?" asked Emi, strolling over to Nat.

Nat nodded. This morning's session on the beach had done a great job of psyching him up for training. Far from tiring him out, it had actually energised him to do a thousand times better than he had the day before. Ian Fox would be keeping a very close eye on him and he was going to show the gaffer he was up to the pace.

From his first second out on the pitch, Nat got stuck in. He was at the front of the pack for all of the initial running exercises. He was excellent in the passing and dribbling drills and he ran and harried in the two versus one possession and tackling sessions. After this, Stan Evans called the four strikers, the two goalies, Emi and the Wildman to the far goalmouth, while the others worked with Fox.

"Right, lads," began Evans, "we've got Celtic tomorrow night and, as you all know, they've got Angus Reakin and Paul Smithfield in central defence."

Nat swallowed nervously.

"The boss and I have picked up on something which we want to work on."

Nat and Emi exchanged an interested glance.

"They know we'll be playing four-four-two, just like them," said Evans. "So Reakin and Smithfield will each pick up one of our strikers."

Nat nodded. He'd seen them do exactly this with the Lazio forwards in last night's game. Being marked by either of them was a daunting prospect.

"However," went on Evans, "there's a chink in their armour. At corners and set pieces Reakin will always stay with his man, but Smithfield sometimes hangs back. Having a massive figure like him on the goal line is always a useful blocking device, but when he does stay back, the striker he's marking gets some legroom. We want to exploit that tomorrow night."

"Sounds good," nodded Dennis Jensen.

"So," carried on Evans, "Graham and Jack will take turns in goal now – five minutes on, five minutes off. Adilson, take these balls. I want you to take corners and free kicks first from the left and then from the right. Wildman – you're going to be Angus Reakin. You'll always stick to your man. Emi, you're Smithfield, so mix it up – stay with your opponent half of the time, but the other half hang back on the goal line, OK?"

The Wildman and Emi nodded.

"Strikers, I'm going to rotate you to try you out in all sorts of different combinations. You'll all get a chance to be marked by the Wildman and Emi, or in this case, Angus Reakin and Paul Smithfield. Nat and Dennis – you're on first."

Adilson started pumping balls into the area, with the Wildman pretending to be Reakin and Emi pretending to be Smithfield. When Nat was being marked by the Wildman/Reakin, he hardly got a sniff of the ball. But when he and Jensen switched and Emi/Smithfield became his marker, he found that every other ball he suddenly had the freedom to dart around the penalty area and this allowed him to get in a couple of decent shots and then score with a crisp volley past Graham Dalston. Seeing the ball hit the back of the net was deeply reassuring.

Evans kept them at it for forty-five minutes, drilling them again and again to take advantage of Emi/Smithfield's goal line hang-backs. Sometimes his presence on the line denied a goal-scoring opportunity, but at other times it enabled all four strikers to bag some goals. Evans and Fox were right on the money – it was an area Rangers would be stupid not to look at. By the end of the session Nat had scored nine goals and his confidence was rising rapidly, yesterday's poor showing a fading memory.

During the five-a-sides in the last portion of training Nat was totally up with the pace, exchanging passes with speed and accuracy. In his second game, he swerved past Paulo Carigio and smacked the ball with some wicked spin past Jack Bell into the net.

"Spot on!" shouted Evans from the touchline. Fox

stood next to him, the trademark inscrutable expression on his face. Nat had another shot parried and scored again a few seconds before the end with a blistering long-range shot. The Wildman patted him on the back after the final whistle.

"You're fired up today, kid, aren't you?"

Nat gave him a relieved smile. He knew he'd done well, but he wasn't going to rest on that – he'd try even harder in training tomorrow. He so badly wanted to play his way onto the subs bench for the Celtic game tomorrow night.

It was only when training was over that Nat allowed himself the chance to take a look round the stadium. The stands were empty – the man in the blue suit wasn't there. He breathed a sigh of relief and went in to join the others.

Nat was pretty sure that, though he'd performed very well in training, Ian Fox wasn't going to rush over and shower him with praise. And he was right. The boss gave him nothing, not even an encouraging nod. Fox could dish out criticism, but he was very sparing with congratulations – too many years at the coalface of football life had made him extremely wary of gushing sentimentality. Adilson, however, came up to Nat and shook his hand so hard he almost yanked his arm out of its socket.

"Excellent goals, Nat," he grinned. "Get a couple like that against Celtic tomorrow and we'll be sorted!"

"Cheers," replied Nat, grateful for the acknowledgement.

It's nice to be appreciated!

When the players emerged from the El Mar Stadium, Nat spotted a small group of Spanish teenagers, wearing their country's shirts and laughing among themselves.

One of them, wearing a red and yellow baseball cap and a huge fake gold medallion, shouted to his mates and they scuttled over to Nat, Emi and Kelvin.

"Alright, guys," said Emi jovially.

"If you make it to the final, you will play Talorca," said the boy wearing the baseball cap.

"How do you know Talorca will make it to the final?" asked Kelvin, with a broad smile on his face.

The guy laughed. "Of course we will make it to the final. We will soon be Spanish champions – you will see!"

"If we make it to the final, I reckon we'll beat you!" replied Emi.

The lad quickly translated this conversation into Spanish. His friends laughed loudly and said something back.

"They say, 'In your dreams'," reported the boy.

"We beat Manchester United a few weeks ago," Nat pointed out.

"I know," replied the boy, "but Manchester don't have Alberto Tieras, do they?"

"We've dealt with far tougher players in our time," grinned Emi. "Tieras is a kitten compared to some of them!"

"We'll see about that!" said the Spanish boy, reaching out to shake Emi's hand. All of his friends then insisted upon shaking Emi, Nat and Kelvin's hands and after that, posing for photos with all three of them, and getting them to autograph several pieces of paper, two canvas bags, a notebook and the baseball-cap boy's left shoe.

When the team bus pulled up alongside the kerb, the Spanish boys shouted their thanks and farewells and made off, delighted with the autographs and photos they'd accumulated and still utterly convinced that if Rangers made it to the final, they'd come up against Talorca and get completely battered.

"Do you reckon we've got a chance to make it to the final?" asked Kelvin as the coach pulled away and set out for the team hotel.

Nat didn't say anything. He was focusing solely on tomorrow night's Celtic game and achieving the thing that he craved the most – some precious minutes on the pitch.

CHAPTER 11
Hidden from Prying Eyes

"I've brought you some extra blankets, more food and scissors to cut your hair."

Carlos grabbed the loaf of bread Rudy brought out of his rucksack, tore a great chunk off it and ravenously tucked in. The barn they were sitting in was a couple of miles off the nearest back road.

"Are you sure no one followed you here?" demanded Carlos, in between mouthfuls.

"Absolutely," Rudy replied. "I hardly saw any other vehicles for the whole journey."

"Good," nodded Carlos. "Is everything arranged?"

"Tomorrow night we make our move," nodded Rudy. "I've staked out the place for the last five nights and the pattern is always the same. There are two guards. During their changeover they have a cup of coffee in the hut round the side of the building. This takes a minimum of ten minutes – on some nights it's more like fourteen."

"Excellent," said Carlos, taking a slug from the bottle of water Rudy had provided.

After Carlos had found a phone in the village the previous night, he'd run back to the ditch and awaited Rudy's arrival. It was pitch-dark by then and the headlights of Rudy's vehicle were the only points of light on the deserted country road.

They'd gone fifteen miles when Rudy pulled up, opened a metal gate at the side of the road and drove down a bumpy trail that ended next to a dilapidated barn. Rudy had visited the barn on several occasions at different times of day to be absolutely certain it was never used.

Rudy killed the engine and they got out. Flicking on his torch, Rudy pulled back the creaky barn door. It had obviously once been a place where animals had been kept because there were old sacks of animal feed on the ground and a couple of pens. But that had been years ago.

Carlos had nodded his approval of the place. "There will be scores of police out looking for me," he said. "They'll be checking every place I've ever hung out. The escape will be a massive embarrassment to the prison service and they'll want me back inside as soon as possible."

"I know," nodded Rudy. "The story's been everywhere. This place is perfect, at least for the moment. When we've finished the project we'll have to sort you out something more permanent. People can properly 'disappear' if they get a total identity makeover. We'll give it our best shot."

"Let's not worry about that now," replied Carlos. "It's one day at a time for the minute."

Rudy nodded.

"OK," said Carlos. "Make your move out of here and I'll see you tomorrow night."

A full twenty-four hours had passed since then without Carlos being detected. The story of his break-out had been on the radio and in the press, but had quickly dropped down the news agenda when a massive forest fire broke out near some farmland, and public sector workers announced a strike over pay and working conditions.

Rudy turned away, ready to leave Carlos for the second day, when he remembered something. Reaching into his jacket pocket, he pulled out a photo and handed it to Carlos.

"This is the guy?" asked Carlos, shining the torch onto the print.

Rudy nodded.

Carlos studied the face. "What's his name?" he asked.

Rudy paused for a second and then said in a cold, clear tone, "Nat Dixon."

CHAPTER 12
Talking it Out

The atmosphere back at the hotel was relaxed. Training had gone well, the players were getting used to the heat and the facilities were great. After a long lunch, Nat spent the afternoon relaxing by the pool, swimming and playing several games of table tennis and snooker with Kelvin and Adilson. Nat was really enjoying himself, so the hours flew by and suddenly it was supper time. Alcohol wasn't banned by the club, but everyone knew Ian Fox's attitude towards excessive drinking, so a few of the players had a single beer with the meal, while the rest settled for soft drinks.

After eating, Nat played another couple of games of snooker with Adilson and then wandered to the hotel lobby, intending to use the quietness of the place to phone his dad. It was empty save for an elderly couple enjoying a cup of coffee and a large, suited businessman with oversize dark glasses talking on his mobile. Nat spotted Emi sitting by himself on an armchair next to a low coffee table. A bottle of lemonade was sitting there, half drunk. Emi looked serious and was busy sending a text on his mobile.

Nat strolled over and sat down on the armchair opposite. He waited until Emi had finished texting and then spoke.

"Hey Emi, what's up?"

Emi looked up. "Oh, hi Nat. I've just been texting my mum. My dad's not well."

"What's wrong with him?"

"He was rushed into hospital this morning in Yamoussoukro – that's the capital of Ivory Coast. He complained of chest pains last night – he and my mother thought it was just indigestion. It went away and he got a good night's sleep. But this morning it was a whole lot worse and he also got these shooting pains up his left arm."

"Was it a heart attack?" asked Nat quietly.

"The doctors thought so at first, but they ran some tests on him and it wasn't."

"So what was it?"

"They don't know," sighed Emi. "They've kept him in for more tests. My mum is really worried. She's convinced he's at death's door. But my father is a fighter and keeps telling her not to be ridiculous. He says if he was facing death he'd know about it, and that these are definitely not his last breaths."

"When will they know what's going on?" asked Nat.

"No one knows," replied Emi. "But I'm worried and

it's tough not being there with them. A part of me feels I should get on a plane right now."

"Why don't you? The gaffer would totally understand."

"I know, but my dad would kill me! He's so proud of what I do that if he thought I'd shirked away from any team duties even for a day or two he'd never let me hear the last of it. But look – here I am going on about my dad, when you lost your mum. I shouldn't be complaining about it."

"Of course you should," smiled Nat sympathetically. "You're worried and you *need* to talk about it. It's natural."

They sat in silence for a minute or so.

"Nat," said Emi softly, "did your mum die of a heart attack?"

Nat felt a jolt in his chest. He'd told Emi and Kelvin that she'd died but he hadn't given them any details.

"No," sighed Nat. "She was killed in a car crash."

"My God!" whispered Emi, "I'm so sorry."

"It was awful," Nat murmured, "the worst thing that could ever happen to you as a kid – your mum being taken away from you in such appalling circumstances. My dad was so crushed by the whole thing that we packed up and left England. If I hadn't been discovered by Stan Evans in the States, I'd probably still be out there."

"Do you still miss her?" asked Emi quietly.

"Every day," said Nat, "but it's much, much better than

it used to be. It's been so long that I'm used to it now. There'll often be moments when I want to tell her about something I've done, but the pain isn't so great now. It's still there, but I can live with it."

They sat in silence for a few moments, both of their eyebrows furrowed in thought.

"I can't believe you had to go through all of that," said Emi.

"But come on, Emi. You're going through a rough time at the moment. It must be really difficult for *you*."

"So should I go back?" asked Emi.

"Why don't you speak to one of the doctors, gauge their opinion about your dad's condition. You can make your mind up after that."

"Good idea," replied Emi. "I'll do that."

The conversation then lightened up and they switched to chatting about the Celtic game. Nat felt a pulse of relief in his chest. Talking to Emi about his mum hadn't been so bad. Emi was a really sympathetic listener and at the moment he could really relate to Nat's loss. Maybe Nat needed to talk about his mother a bit more – maybe it would help the healing process if he got things off his chest from time to time.

They were talking about the hulks of Angus Reakin and Paul Smithfield an hour later when Ian Fox and Stan Evans strolled into the lobby.

"OK, you two!" called Fox, marching over to them. "It's nine thirty. Time for bed!"

"Who says so?" laughed Emi.

"Me!" stated the gaffer.

"Yes, boss," said Emi, as he and Nat stood.

"Good," said Fox with satisfaction. "Now get some sleep and you'll be fresh for the morning. "

Nat phoned Inés to tell her he was going to get a cab back.

"You don't need to," she replied. "It's part of the deal. The club are paying me to have you as my guest, remember? Let me come and get you."

"I'm fine, honestly. There are plenty of cabs outside."

"OK, if you're sure."

Nat and Emi went outside to get taxis. Their hosts lived in opposite directions, so Emi got into one cab and Nat climbed into another. In faltering Spanish he had to give the driver Inés's address three times before the man understood him. The taxi had only just set off when his mobile rang.

"Hi Dad."

"How was training today?"

"It was much better than yesterday."

"That's great. You all set for tomorrow night?"

"I don't know if I'll get on."

"You're bound to feature at some stage."

"Ian Fox never reveals what he's thinking. I might not even get on the subs bench."

"Don't be mad! Think of what you did against Man United."

"I think he's forgotten that now."

"Well, whatever happens, don't forget how you got there – by sheer hard work and determination."

"And some major lying," quipped Nat.

"OK," laughed Dave, "that as well. One of the lads at work has hundreds of cable channels and he says that one of them is showing tomorrow's match."

"Nice one."

"Where are you now?"

"I'm in a cab on my way back to the villa."

"Good move. Hope tomorrow turns out well."

"Cheers Dad, catch you later."

The taxi driver took a slightly circuitous route, but Nat wasn't prepared to try and have an argument in his weak Spanish so he just paid the fare.

As he walked towards the villa, he passed the window of José's room. The curtains were open and Nat spied José sitting on his bed with a look of intense concentration on his face. At first Nat assumed he was reading a magazine or a newspaper but when he edged a bit closer he saw that he was counting some bank notes. And this wasn't a small pocket-money type pile. This was a huge wad.

Nat frowned and hurried on, making sure that José hadn't spotted him. Where on earth did José get that kind of cash? He didn't have a job at the minute and it certainly wouldn't be Inés's money – she'd said she didn't earn that much from teaching and that they just about got by on her salary and a small pension left by her husband.

Nat stepped inside, mulling this over. Could someone have lent it to him? Or maybe he'd just sold something valuable on eBay or another trading site? But what? And did Inés know about this money?

Nat got changed for bed, still thinking about these questions. As he closed his eyes, his mind switched from José's money to tomorrow night's Celtic game. He now understood why some players were so reluctant to retire. There was something so incredible about being part of a set-up at a club like Hatton Rangers. All of the players battled for each other – it was an amazing camaraderie and one you'd do very well to ever better. He closed his eyes and pictured the El Mar Stadium, the pitch bathed in rays of floodlight as it had been on Sunday night for the Lazio v Celtic game.

Come on, Fox – give me a chance out there!

CHAPTER 13
Burglar Territory

Ray Swinton handed over the money to his waiter and left the restaurant. He'd only arrived in Talorca three hours before, but after checking in at his hotel (which was a five minute walk from the one the Hatton Rangers players were staying in) he'd already interviewed the Talorca manager, written up a match preview of the Hatton Rangers v Celtic game and emailed it to his editor, and placed a couple of bets on the game. He'd also enjoyed a good meal and a glass of decent Spanish wine.

Hatton Rangers had always been Swinton's team – he'd followed them as a kid, and as a journalist on the *Sunday Crest*, he reported on pretty much every game and going-on at the club, as well as covering quite a few other Premier League teams. He'd avidly followed each twist and swerve of last season's nail-biting campaign, culminating in Nat Dixon's glorious last-gasp winner against Manchester United. Nat Dixon had given Swinton an exclusive on the Chris Webb match-fixing story, which had added thousands of sales to the *Crest* and had garnered Swinton some praise from the paper's editor Hugh Asquith.

The Dixon lad fascinated Swinton. Not only because of his part in thwarting Webb's ugly dealings or because of his amazing pace, excellent passing and thunderous shot. No, Swinton had also received an anonymous tip-off from Brazil that Dixon was younger than the sixteen years both he and his club claimed him to be. Swinton would have gone with this story if it hadn't been for Dixon delivering him the Webb scoop. He'd promised Nat that he'd go nowhere near this 'age' story again, but if he ever got solid proof that it was true, he'd be more than tempted to have another look at it. After all, how often did you get an underage player plying their trade in the Premier League?

Swinton arrived back at his hotel and took the lift to the fourth floor in excellent spirits. He was looking forward to catching a late-night Spanish football show on TV and having a nightcap from the minibar. He was out here in Spain at his newspaper's expense. Life could taste sweet.

So he was totally taken aback when he found two Spanish policemen outside room 112 – his room. One of them said something to him in Spanish.

"Er . . . I'm sorry," replied Swinton. "Do you speak English?"

The first policeman looked blank, but the second

one stepped forward. "Is this your room?" he asked in heavily-accented English.

Swinton nodded.

"Unfortunately your room and the two rooms on either side of it have been broken into," explained the policeman. "We have someone inside at the moment looking for fingerprints."

"I don't believe it!" exclaimed Swinton, "I've only been in the country for a few hours."

"I'm sorry, sir. We got a call from the manager twenty minutes ago. The doors had been forced. We came here immediately."

Before Swinton could reply, a man emerged from his room, holding a small case and shaking his head – there were no fingerprints. He spoke to both officers then headed off down the corridor.

"You may go into your room now," said the English-speaking officer. "The hotel will fix your door. When you have had a look around we will need to ask you about what has been taken."

"Fine," said Swinton, walking past them and entering his room.

It was in a state. The cupboards and the writing desk had been turned out, the bedding was on the floor and his duty free bag had been emptied, with several bottles of spirits now missing. Luckily Swinton had had his wallet and passport with him. It could have been much worse.

And then a thought struck him. He span round and

looked at the bedside table. He'd placed three of his most treasured and precious possessions on there – his irreplaceable notebooks. He felt a bolt of shock in his chest when he saw to his dismay that they were no longer there. This was far worse than a few missing bottles of vodka. This was serious. It had big implications, not just for him, but for other people as well. And one of those people was Nat Dixon.

CHAPTER 14
Crashed Out

At breakfast Inés was quiet. She read the papers and kept sipping from a small cup of coffee. José wasn't around. Nat had some toast and orange juice. After a while Inés folded the newspaper and put it down on the table.

"There's something I want to tell you," she said.

Nat looked at her expectantly.

"It's about José."

Nat looked back towards the door, expecting José to be hovering there.

"Don't worry," said Inés, "he's gone to Almería this morning – chasing some kind of lead about a possible job with an architect's firm. He really is trying."

Nat pursed his lips, waiting for her to cut to the chase.

Inés sighed. "It's about him storming out yesterday. I should try and explain."

"You don't need to," said Nat.

"I know, but I want to."

"OK," replied Nat.

"You know I told you about my husband's crash?"

Nat nodded.

"Well José was involved in the crash too."

Nat's eyes widened. *They were on that motorbike together!*

"They crashed into a tree. My husband took the full force of the impact. José was thrown onto the road."

"Did he get hurt?"

"Oh yes," nodded Inés sadly. "He was heavily concussed and broke several bones in his right leg and ankle. He was in hospital for a couple of weeks."

"But he recovered?"

"Yes, but unfortunately it put paid to his playing career."

Nat raised an eyebrow. *His playing career?*

"José was on course to become a professional player, Nat, just like you. He'd been with Talorca FC youth teams since the age of eight. The injuries he sustained on his leg and ankle meant he would never play again."

Nat took a deep breath and blew out his cheeks. "I can't believe it," he said.

"I know, it's a tragedy," sighed Inés. "He was a very promising player – a midfielder. Everyone at Talorca rated him very highly. But then the crash happened and that was all extinguished in one breath. That's why he's gloomy a lot of the time and why he feels so negative about Talorca. He's just very crushed inside. It will take him many years to come to terms with it."

They sat in silence, Nat trying to absorb this new and shocking information.

"It must be hard for José having me stay here," mused Nat. "I mean, I'm a professional player staying in his house. You must have thought about that when you agreed to have me to stay."

"Of course I did," replied Inés, "but when I mentioned it to José he said it was a good idea."

"Really?" exclaimed Nat with surprise.

"He seemed very keen. I don't know, maybe it's some kind of test for him – if he could deal with having a footballer to stay, he could further get to grips with the accident and the fact that his career was ruined by it."

Nat mulled this over. He knew that if the tables were turned and he was the one whose career was over, he'd never in a million years want a player staying at his house. It would be too painful. Maybe Inés was right, though, maybe José wanted to test himself.

"Anyway," said Inés, "now I've told you and I'm glad that I did. I just wanted to let you know about José's sensitivity with regard to Talorca FC."

"Thanks for telling me," replied Nat, pleased that she'd confided in him.

"We'll set out for El Mar in a couple of minutes, OK?" said Inés.

"That's great," replied Nat.

He headed off to his room to collect his things. The door to José's room was open a fraction. Nat peered round it, half expecting the huge wad of cash José had been handling to be on his bed or desk, but there was no money anywhere, save for a couple of coins on the floor.

CHAPTER 15
The Real Thing

"Nat, can you come over here please?" called Stan Evans.

Training had just finished and Nat was satisfied with his contribution. He'd worked hard during all of the runs and drills and had bagged a couple of decent goals in a seven v seven game at the end of the session. Far from being miles from the standards set by others, he'd given an excellent account of himself. Surely Ian Fox saw that and accepted he'd improved his game?

Nat walked over to Evans as the other players headed back into the changing room.

"I want to do a bit of extra work with you today," explained Evans.

"OK," nodded Nat. This wasn't unusual. Evans often asked a player, or a couple of them, to hang back and go over some drills or work on some tactical planning.

"What are we going to focus on?" asked Nat.

"Well, the gaffer and I have been talking about you," said Evans, "and we'd both like to see a bit more of the physical side of your game. I know that because of your age you're nowhere near fully-developed, but you're well built enough to compete in this aspect of the game."

"Fine," nodded Nat.

"It's especially important because Reakin and Smithfield are very tough defenders to play against," went on Evans. "We don't know yet if you'll get a game at all, but if you do, those two will be throwing their weight around big time to show our attackers who is king of the Celtic penalty area. So this is what you and I are going to do. You're going to dribble into the penalty area and I'm going to be waiting there for you. I'm going to use my upper body strength to try and outmuscle you to the ball. Call it a barge, an enthusiastic challenge, or a despicable piece of naked aggression – it doesn't really matter. I want to see you withstanding these challenges without going down."

"I've got it," nodded Nat.

Evans threw Nat a ball and retreated into the penalty area of the goal nearest to them.

Nat dropped the ball onto the turf and began to run towards the area. Evans had placed himself ten yards inside the box, directly in front of goal. And he launched himself at Nat as if he really meant it. Nat felt the full force of the impact and went crashing onto the ground, his shoulder feeling as if it had just been attacked with an iron bar.

Evans put out his hand and helped Nat up.

"Let's go again," said Evans, "and this time don't

just take the impact, react against it. Use my own barge against me."

Nat ran at the goal and once again Evans issued another crunching challenge that floored him. He got up, shook himself down and lined up another run. This time, Evan's challenge knocked him off balance but he stayed on his feet. He could see what Evans meant about using his opponent's strength against them. If he met the barge halfway and shoved back with all his power he could maintain his equilibrium.

He went down on his fourth go but stayed up for his fifth. On his sixth attempt, he gritted his teeth and ordered himself to go in hard, meet fire with fire, get round Evans. As he raced into the box he was ready for Evans and took the force of his challenge with an equally strong movement of his upper body. A split second after impact, he had swerved round Evans, the ball still at his feet.

"Excellent!" shouted Evans. "That's more like it!"

For the next half hour, Nat and Evans stayed out there. Evans switched his position in the penalty area and kept challenging Nat. Nat was knocked over quite a few times, both his shoulders and his chest taking mighty knocks, but by the end he was staying on his feet more and more, and was beginning to relish the face-offs.

"OK, we'll stop there," puffed Evans. "You did very well. I know it will be different in the actual match, but stick to what we've just worked on and you should be OK."

"I'll try," answered Nat.

"Just remember," said Evans as they walked back to the changing room, "every moment spent with this club is another step on a gigantic learning curve. Even the most experienced players still pick things up. You look at the Wildman – he's always listening, always learning."

Nat spent the afternoon in the team hotel, swimming again and drawing three-three with Kelvin in a hard-fought table tennis contest. The players ate a light supper of grilled fish and vegetables, washed down with water and a healthy protein charge of assorted nuts. Nat sat between Emi and Nicky Sinclair, and although everyone was chatting and cracking jokes, Nat's mind was on that night's match. He was a bit more confident now that he'd make the subs bench, but you never knew with Ian Fox. Talk about keeping your positional cards close to your chest! Mind you, why would Stan Evans put extra time into getting him physically ready for facing Reakin and Smithfield if he wasn't actually going to play against them in some capacity?

He'd have to wait a bit longer for this information, though. Fox had told them he'd only be revealing the team over at the El Mar Stadium, a couple of hours before kick off. When it was finally time to board the team bus, Nat felt the tense anticipation rising within him, and he elected to sit by himself, picturing the two Celtic centre-backs in his mind, and seeing himself challenging them in the way he'd practised with Stan Evans in training that morning.

Inside the changing room, Nat was jittery.

"Alright?" asked the Wildman, coming over and sitting down on the bench next to him.

"Yeah," lied Nat. "I'm fine.

The Wildman looked him in the eye. "Are you sure?"

Nat nodded, trying to look confident.

"Don't forget what I told you," said the Wildman. "I still get nervous before every game, especially big ones, like tonight. I know it's only one match and that no one will die if I don't play well, but that doesn't stop the adrenalin flowing, OK?"

"Sure," replied Nat.

The gaffer's voice then cut across the changing room.

"Listen up," said Fox and instantly all conversations stopped, as eighteen players sat down on the benches, awaiting the most important announcement of the trip so far. Nat felt the muscles in his stomach tense even further.

"I know lots of the big teams back home are rotating their squads heavily during their pre-season games to try out new blood and new formations," said Fox, "but my intention is to stick to a pretty firm starting eleven wherever possible. I will tinker, and of course there'll be plenty of substitute appearances, but I'm looking to build a strong base. If we can get the team right out here it will be excellent preparation for the new season back home.

Just look at the national sides that go into tournaments *without* a stable line-up – more often than not they act like headless beasts, eleven disconnected parts battling each other."

Nat felt a twist of hope inside. He'd been on top form in the last two training sessions and he'd ended the season on a high. Dennis Jensen was definitely at the front of the striker queue, with Robbie Clarke just behind him. Nicky Sinclair was surely the fourth choice forward? So that should place Nat as first reserve striker, shouldn't it? Mind you, Celtic were very physical opponents. Would Ian Fox agree that Nat was in any way ready for facing them?

"OK," went on Fox. "In goal will be Dalston. At left-back, Young; right-back, Bartlett; with centre-backs, the Wildman and Adeyo."

Jack Bell looked hurt but no one else raised an eyebrow at Dalston's inclusion – he was the senior player and had performed well out here in training so far. There was no surprise at Fox's choice of back four either. They were the bedrock of the team – unless one of them got badly injured or left the club, they'd be staying put. Midfield was going to be interesting, though. The two central midfielders Paulo Carigio and Dean Jobson had a tempestuous relationship. It was connected to the definition of their roles. They both loved attacking but weren't so keen on tracking back and shielding the back four. This had led to a lot of tension in the last few months, which had boiled up as the season drew to a dramatic climax, particularly after the two-one defeat against Tottenham when they really went for each other in the dressing room.

So Nat was a little bit surprised to hear both of their names called out by Ian Fox. He'd have thought that Fox might try each of them playing alongside Jermaine Clifton (who was on excellent form) – maybe one in the first half, the other in the second half – or give them each one game – say, Carigio against Celtic and Jobson against Lazio.

"Alongside Carigio and Jobson will be Adilson on the left of midfield, and Sacrois on the right."

Nat felt his nerves start buzzing into overdrive. Now it was the strikers' turn.

"Upfront will be Jensen and . . . Clarke."

Even though he'd expected this, he still felt a pang of envy, but Nat made himself smile and he gave Robbie Clarke a thumbs-up.

"The other seven of you will all be on the subs bench," announced Fox, his gaze lingering on Nat's for a couple of seconds.

What a relief. At least I make the cut!

With twenty minutes to go until kick off, all eighteen players went out to warm up on the pitch. The stadium was already filling up and in the far left-hand corner was a group of about three hundred Hatton Rangers fans. The Rangers squad ran over and clapped them, a welcome that was delightedly returned by the fans. Then it was passing and dribbling drills led by Stan Evans, as the stadium rapidly filled up. Just as for the Celtic v Lazio game, local people were keen to see the match, even though their team, El Mar, weren't playing.

"Alright, lads," shouted Evans, checking his watch ten minutes later. "Back inside."

In the changing room the first eleven ditched their tracksuits for their kit, while the subs kept theirs on.

"I'm sure the boss will give you a run out," whispered Stan Evans, slapping Nat on the back.

"Thanks," nodded Nat, grateful for Evans's positivity. It wasn't long before the two teams were lining up in the tunnel, nodding hellos to each other. Celtic had won a toss earlier in the evening and so were in their home kit, while Hatton Rangers were in their away kit of black shirts, black shorts and black-and-white striped socks.

The subs hung back behind the two lines and followed them out when the teams strode onto the pitch. They were met by a wall of sound and the twenty-two first choice players lined up on the touchline for formal introductions and handshakes with local dignitaries, while the subs hit the benches.

"Do you reckon you'll get a game tonight?" asked Jermaine Clifton, sitting down next to Nat.

"No idea," replied Nat with a shrug of his shoulders. "What about you?"

"No one can ever second-guess the boss," smiled Clifton.

Nat liked Jermaine. Not only was he an excellent player, he was also very into team spirit and was genuinely delighted for other players when they did well. Nat wanted to become a bit more like that – at the minute a part of him really wanted Jensen or Clarke to have a bad game so he'd have a chance of coming off the subs bench and getting to play.

Nat turned to focus on the pitch. The Hatton Rangers players were warming up on the half of the pitch to his left. Emi and the Wildman were heading balls to each other in the penalty area, Dennis Jensen and Robbie Clarke were lobbing balls at Graham Dalston in the Rangers goal, while Adilson and Kelvin were exchanging quick-fire, low balls that skimmed over the turf. Dean Jobson, Paulo Carigio, Pierre Sacrois and Andy Young were standing in a square, playing keepy-uppy.

I wish I was out there!

On the right side of the pitch, the Celtic captain Angus Reakin was walking round his players, slapping them on the back, issuing words of encouragement and shaking his fist at them. Reakin really was a 'players' player', loved and respected by his teammates. He had that spirit of utter belief in his own abilities and in those of his team, and he would do almost anything to lead Celtic to victory.

Nat then checked out Celtic's tiny but hugely skilful right-sided midfielder – Gavin Clyde. He was smashing in shots at their gigantic keeper Bruce Collins. Just outside the Celtic area were their central midfield pairing of

Nigel Flort and Neil Trent, both very experienced players, with plenty of European games under their belts. Strikers Ilio Campdora and Jimmy Doode were rifling passes at each other, while left-back Rob Storey and right-back Davey Cathcart were going on short, fast sprints. Would Cathcart's forays into the Rangers half allow Rangers players to exploit the space he left behind?

The Romanian referee checked his watch, consulted with his assistants and blew his whistle. The game was on.

CHAPTER 16
The Match Comes to Life

Celtic kicked off and played the ball straight to Gavin Clyde. He exchanged a one-two with Ilio Campdora, who started a move that ended with Clyde firing a thunderous shot just over the bar, much to Graham Dalston's relief. Ian Fox was up in a second and into the technical area, screaming at Dean Jobson for letting Clyde outpace him in the middle third of the park.

Hatton Rangers then launched their own attack, with Carigio threading a neat pass through to Adilson, whose shot from the edge of the Celtic area was parried by Collins. The Celtic goalie whacked the ball back towards the centre circle. This was followed in quick succession by a scuffed attempt by Pierre Sacrois, and a curling lob from the Celtic left-back Rob Storey, which grazed the post.

The next twenty minutes followed this to and fro pattern, seeing some decent attempts on goal from both teams, which forced Dalston and Collins to make some excellent saves. Robbie Clarke and Dennis Jensen both had good efforts parried by Collins. It was great to see Graham Dalston pulling off stops like this. It meant that ex-keeper Chris Webb could be consigned to the dustbin of history.

There then followed a frantic five minutes for Hatton Rangers, during which Celtic launched several blistering attacks, forcing Rangers to defend very deep. A Gavin Clyde volley that looked like it was going in was intercepted by a diving header from the Wildman and then a Campdora header was athletically tipped over the bar by Dalston, which earned him several slaps on the back from relieved teammates.

But then, on thirty-nine minutes, Celtic conceded a penalty.

Hatton Rangers were awarded a free kick on the right edge of the penalty area after Dennis Jensen was fouled by Clyde. Adilson strode over to take the kick. Reakin picked up Jensen and stuck to him like a powerful adhesive. But Smithfield positioned himself on the goal line exactly as Stan Evans had predicted. This allowed Robbie Clarke to hang back unmarked, and when Adilson hit the ball short to Clarke and Clarke swung his leg back to hit it, Gavin Clyde grabbed his shirt and Robbie Clarke went down. Clarke was an honest player – he very rarely dived. So when he hit the turf, the referee had no hesitation in awarding Hatton Rangers a penalty.

"YESSSS!" yelled Nat, leaping to his feet with the rest of the Hatton Rangers bench.

"You must be joking!" Angus Reakin bawled at the referee, following him to the edge of the penalty area. When he tapped the ref on the arm, the official swung round and held aloft a yellow card. Paul Smithfield quickly grabbed Reakin and led the Celtic captain away.

Nat had taken the last Rangers penalty in the game against Manchester United. True, he'd hit the bar and scored on a rebound, but he still wished he were out there to take this one. However, it was Adilson who dug a small hole with the toe of his boot before placing the ball down, ignoring the Celtic left-back Rob Storey, who had come over to talk to him, in an attempt to put him off. Bruce Collins in the Celtic goal had a bit of form at penalty-saving – he'd made an incredible save two seasons ago from an AC Milan penalty in the dying minutes of a Champions League game at the San Siro.

But Nat had every confidence in Adilson. The Brazilian star was not only a superb technical player, he was also very calm when it came to set pieces.

Go on Adilson – bury it!

The Celtic supporters whistled and booed far louder than their small numbers should allow, willing Adilson to miss or Collins to save. Adilson stepped back a few metres and then took his run up. He hit the ball sweetly, high and to the goalie's left, but Collins made an incredibly athletic leap, arching his back like a leopard in flight, and pushed the ball round the post. The Celtic fans went crazy, screaming and yelling and singing Collins's name. The

Celtic keeper gave them a wave of thanks. The Rangers fans fell silent for a few seconds, before chanting loudly in an attempt to rouse their players to fight back.

Adilson stood rooted to the penalty spot, amazed that Collins had managed to deny him. The Wildman ran over to him and put an arm round his shoulders, ordering him to immediately wipe it off his memory disc and get on with the rest of the game.

"Forget it, son!" shouted Ian Fox, sleeves rolled up, his face animated as he stood at the edge of the technical area.

Adilson did as he was told. The penalty miss ignited him and for the next five minutes he was in almost constant possession of the ball, spraying passes, dodging round defenders and shooting from all angles. But there was no goal.

As the clock wound down, both sides began to play very defensively, keen not to concede before half-time. So when the whistle went, the score stood at nil-nil, and Nat made a beeline for Adilson.

"You were so unlucky with the penalty," he said. "It was a beauty. Collins did amazingly to get to it."

"Thanks," smiled Adilson. "I really thought it was going in."

"That's just the way it goes," said Stan Evans, joining them. "However good your technique is, you can't score them all."

Back in the changing room, Ian Fox waited for all of

his players to grab a drink and go to the toilet before he began his half-time talk.

"OK, lads," he began. "That wasn't a bad first half. At the start we gave away possession far too easily, but we became more disciplined and we fully deserved the penalty. Bad luck, Adilson. Even I missed a couple in my time."

There were laughs round the room.

Adilson nodded to thank the boss for this show of support.

"In the second half," went on Fox, "I want you to play the ball more to feet. Davey Cathcart, their right-back, looks like he's carrying some kind of injury. If he's still on for the next forty-five, take advantage of that. Let's get some balls down that channel and hit some crosses in. Wildman and Emi, I want both of you to press up at set plays – put some pressure on their back four. Kelvin you stay back to cover them. OK?"

The Wildman, Emi and Kelvin nodded.

Ten minutes later, everyone filed out for the second half.

But in spite of Fox's words, Hatton Rangers didn't keep possession for long. Fortunately for them, Celtic were just as bad and the match started to become a scrappy affair. Both teams chose safe passes instead of trying to break through to the opposition goal. But on fifty-eight minutes the game reignited. Gavin Clyde smashed an incredibly forceful long-range free kick towards the Rangers goal.

The Wildman, who was standing on the line, just managed to head it to safety.

That free kick and the close escape were a wake-up call for Rangers and they started putting some decent passing moves together. Adilson had a half chance after he picked up the ball in the Celtic D, but he scuffed his shot and it rolled into the hands of Bruce Collins. Dean Jobson then headed a corner wide.

However, Ian Fox wasn't satisfied. As the clock passed the seventieth minute mark he turned to Nat. "I'm taking Carigio off. Four-four-two isn't working. I've given it most of the game but if we're to take the three points, we need to get amongst them. I want to move to four-three-three with you and Clarke playing on either side of Jensen – you on the left. You need to put pressure on Davey Cathcart. He's only firing at about eighty per cent. Your speed might undo him. Let everyone know what we're doing, OK?"

"Yes, boss," said Nat, with a great surge of excitement. Stan Evans hurried over to the fourth official to inform him of the change.

As soon as the ball was out of play, the fourth official held up his electronic board with Carigio's number seven in red and Nat's thirty-three in green. Carigio spotted his number and jogged off, exchanging a handshake with Nat. He didn't look too pleased. In fact, he looked as if someone had just uttered a hideous insult to his mother, but Nat didn't have time to think about that. Number thirty-three was now on. It was another chance to play with the grown-ups.

"We're going four-three-three," Nat shouted at the Wildman as he ran onto the pitch. Nat jogged over to Jensen and Clarke to inform them of the switch.

"The gaffer's right to mix things up," nodded Jensen. "We've got to find a way past Reakin and Smithfield. Cathcart is definitely not at full power. We'll get the ball to you, Nat – you make it to the byeline. Robbie and I will get into decent positions for your crosses."

Nat sprinted over to the left side of the pitch. The ref blew his whistle and the throw-in was quickly taken. Nat could smell the freshly-cut grass and was aware of the shouts from the players and the noises from the crowd, but he knew that if he wanted to achieve anything, he had to block all of that out.

For his first five minutes on the pitch, Nat had no possession. But then the Wildman picked him out with a pass from inside the Rangers's penalty area. Nat took the ball in his stride and suddenly he was on his way. Cathcart ran towards him. Nat swerved left and then right to beat his man and left him floundering. He sped on and cut inside to approach the Celtic penalty area. Angus Reakin powered out to challenge him, but Nat spun away from the challenge and lofted the ball over the Celtic captain. It flew into the area. Dennis Jensen reached it with his right boot but his contact was weak and Bruce Collins made an easy save. After this positive move, though, Nat was fired up and he registered Stan Evans yelling encouragement at him.

Three minutes later, Nat was involved again, but was dispossessed by Reakin just before he made it into the penalty area. And then on eighty-four minutes, when Dean Jobson found Nat with a slide rule pass, Nat accelerated past Cathcart and pelted towards the penalty area. Reakin advanced towards him, his giant frame looking over Nat. But remembering the extra work he'd done in training with Evans, Nat launched himself at the oncoming defender. Nat felt his whole body take a direct hit, but although he wobbled, he stayed upright, dragged the ball past Reakin and hit a deviously curling ball into the Celtic penalty area.

Adilson left his marker for dead, and with a fantastic strike volleyed the ball into the top left hand corner of the Celtic net.

"Sensational goal!" screamed Nat, rushing over to Adilson and hugging him.

"Sensational cross!" laughed the Brazilian

The other Rangers players charged over to dish out their thanks, swarming round the goal-scorer and the provider.

"You GENIUS!" bellowed Emi, whacking Nat on the back.

In the technical area, Ian Fox didn't join in with the celebrations. Instead he yelled at his players to get back into their own half and regain their shape. As Nat expected, Celtic weren't going to let in a goal and not respond, so the last five or so minutes saw Celtic piling everyone forward, streaming into the Hatton Rangers penalty area, hitting the bar twice and inspiring a fantastic low save by Graham Dalston.

In the first minute of time added on, Gavin Clyde thumped the ball into the penalty area. Angus Reakin and the Wildman went up together – two humungous players with incredibly strong necks and heads. On this occasion the Wildman came out on top, his thumping header smashing the ball to safety.

And then the referee blew for full-time.

Hatton Rangers one – Celtic nil.

Nat's twenty minutes on the pitch had seemed to last no more than ten seconds. Everything suddenly took on a dreamlike quality. It was as if he were watching himself and the other Rangers players on a fuzzy screen.

"Fantastic work, son!" beamed Stan Evans, coming over and giving Nat a hearty slap on the back and bringing him back to reality. "Not only did you do what the boss asked by taking on Cathcart, you also gave Reakin an excellent run for his money!"

Ian Fox was less effusive with his praise. He walked up to Nat and shook his hand. That was it.

But Nat didn't mind. The high of getting a game was amazingly powerful. The Rangers players, subs and management team ran over to their wildly celebrating fans, to acknowledge their part in the victory.

Back in the changing room, the atmosphere was fantastic – there was nothing like a victory to lift people's spirits. Stan Evans walked round the room, having a word with everyone who'd got a game.

"You, Emi and Kelvin are coming back to the hotel with the rest of us," he told Nat. "We're not going to have a major celebration – you know what the boss is like. We'll just have a few drinks, mainly non-alcoholic ones!"

"Cool," grinned Nat.

The Wildman led the communal singing and it was a full hour before everyone was changed and ready to leave the stadium. There was more singing and shouting on the team bus.

Back at the hotel, Nat and the others got something to eat and drink and sat in one of the hotel's lounges watching highlights of the game on a large TV and cheering wildly when Nat went on his run and Adilson scored.

The father of Kelvin's host family gave Nat a lift back to Inés's place. Inés came out to meet them and she chatted in Spanish to the dad for a few minutes before he bade his goodbyes and left with Kelvin.

"That was a wonderful pass for Adilson's goal!" said Inés delightedly. "I had a great view."

"Did José come?" asked Nat.

She shook her head. "But you won. You must all be so pleased!"

"We are!" smiled Nat. "Celtic are a tough team."

"Well, you must be hungry. Can I fix you something?"

"No thanks. I ate loads back at the hotel."

"Fine. Get a good night's sleep. You'll need it for the Lazio game. They'll be a bigger test than Celtic."

"I agree," nodded Nat. "Lazio will be much tougher."

Nat said goodnight and made for his room. What an amazing night it had been. He'd got another twenty minutes of first team football under his belt and he'd made the assist for Adilson's goal. Ian Fox hadn't run round the changing room chanting Nat's name, but Nat was sure the gaffer would be satisfied with his performance. Fox might give him a longer run out – maybe even bring him on at half-time. And that was definitely something to look forward to.

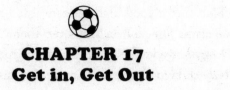

CHAPTER 17
Get in, Get Out

Elsewhere, in the warmth of the Andalusian night, Carlos and Rudy were driving along a narrow road. They didn't speak. In the back seat were two large, empty, black holdalls. If everything went according to plan tonight, the holdalls would be full on the return journey.

They hit the coastal road for a few miles and then turned inland, following a straight road for another few miles before a large industrial estate rose up in the distance. As they approached it, Rudy switched off the headlights and eased his speed to a crawl, using the moonlight as a guide. They parked at a distance of fifty metres and studied the estate for any signs of life. The entire area was bathed in darkness, apart from the odd light or two twinkling in the blackness.

Rudy moved the vehicle forward very slowly, the engine making almost no noise. He turned left onto a service road, which went down the side of the estate. There were ten units, each of which had a loading yard or car park at the back. Rudy stopped in the yard behind the third unit. They got out and took a holdall each from the backseat.

"Remember," whispered Rudy, "we have ten minutes inside."

"If we're fast, no one will know we've been inside or notice anything's gone," agreed Carlos.

Rudy checked his watch. "Seven minutes 'til the guards' changeover," he whispered.

The minutes ticked by. Both of them felt their chests tighten as the adrenaline kicked in. When four minutes were up, Rudy gave Carlos a thumbs-up and they crept over to the giant steel door at the back of the unit. It was locked with two huge padlocks.

Carlos quickly pulled out a small tool for picking locks, and began working on the first padlock, while Rudy kept a lookout. Carlos had been taught well in prison, so he worked smoothly and efficiently. Thirty seconds later, the first padlock fell open. He moved straight on to the second padlock. This one was slightly trickier but he cracked it in just under forty seconds. He pocketed the two padlocks.

Rudy checked his watch and when another minute was up he nodded firmly. Carlos pulled open the steel door and they darted inside, pulling it shut behind them. Rudy took two small headlamps on straps out of his pocket and they affixed these to their foreheads. They hurried down a long aisle on either side of which were huge floor-to-ceiling storage units. Each unit contained boxes and crates of equipment with large signs on the shelves stating what they were.

When they reached the end of the aisle, they came to a walkway which cut between hundreds more shelving units.

Carlos indicated with his thumb for Rudy to go left while he went right. Splitting up would mean they'd locate what they were looking for far quicker. They strode into different aisles, checking the shelves and the labels.

Four minutes later they were both getting tense and frustrated. Their searches had revealed nothing and thin films of sweat were clinging to their foreheads. A couple more fruitless minutes and they were starting to panic. But then Rudy struck gold. He spotted a large sign in front of one of the shelves and a quick swivel of his head torch revealed exactly what he was looking for.

He tried to pull a crate down, but it was out of reach. He turned round and pulled a large box from the opposing shelving unit. Dragging this over, he stepped up onto it and brought down the crate he wanted. He unclipped the lid of the crate and shone his torch at its contents.

Perfect!

Hurriedly he emptied the contents of the crate into his holdall. He stretched up again, pushed the now-empty crate to the back of its row, dragging three full ones in front of it. To the naked eye, nothing had been touched. He then jumped down and replaced the box on the opposite unit.

Hearing footsteps at the end of the aisle, he turned and saw the silhouette of a figure. It was Carlos – he'd tell him the good news. He was about to call out when the figure switched on a torch and Rudy saw with horror that it wasn't Carlos.

It was a guard.

The guard had a large, aggressive-looking dog at his side.

NO!

Rudy checked his watch. There were still three minutes left of the ten. What the hell was the guard doing here?

"HEY!" yelled the guard. A second later, a deafening siren started wailing.

Rudy grabbed his holdall and ran, without a clue of Carlos's whereabouts.

The guard pelted after him, shouting at him to stop. The dog barked ferociously. If the guard let it off the leash, it'd be onto Rudy in seconds.

Rudy reached the end of the aisle and turned right, sprinting as fast as he could, his heart pounding wildly. About forty metres up ahead was the giant steel door. But when he looked round he saw that the guard and the dog were gaining on him.

Frantically, he sped up, pushing himself harder, knowing that to be caught with the contents of the holdall would land him in court and then jail for a very long time.

"STOP!" yelled the guard, his panting breath amplified in the echoing surrounds.

Rudy got to the door a few seconds before the guard. As he ran through, the guard finally let go of the dog – a gigantic Alsatian. The canine crashed towards his back. Rudy yelped in terror as the dog prepared to launch itself into the air with the intention of bringing him down.

But at that exact second there was screeching of tyres as

Carlos swerved the car towards Rudy and kicked open the passenger door.

"Get in!" yelled Carlos.

The dog pounced and Rudy ducked. The Alsatian flew over his head and came crashing down onto the tarmac a few metres in front of Rudy and a few metres short of the vehicle. Rudy swerved round the dog, leapt into the car and slammed the door. The tyres screeched as Carlos hit the accelerator. The dog span round and gave chase, yapping viciously and pounding forward.

"Hey you! Stop there!" screamed the guard, as the dog got ready for another leap.

The dog jumped, but Carlos swerved left and the canine missed the vehicle again. Carlos hurtled round the corner and crashed onto the service road. A few seconds later they skidded back onto the main road.

"You said we had ten minutes minimum!" roared Carlos, the veins on his neck pulsating with fury, as they sped away from the dog, the guard and the screaming sirens.

"I told you – I staked the guards out for five nights!" shouted Rudy. "Ten minutes was the shortest time they took! How was I to know they'd take less time tonight?"

"You weren't," replied Carlos, forcing himself to calm down. "They must have heard us!"

"They couldn't have," countered Rudy. "The guard's hut is a long way from the steel door at the back."

"Alright, alright," said Carlos. "Did you get the stuff?"

"Yes," replied Rudy.

Carlos took a deep breath. "Well done," he nodded. "And you made it look like we didn't take anything? The guy who chased you won't know?"

Rudy thought about the guard appearing at the end of the aisle where he'd found what they were looking for. "He was at least twenty metres away," explained Rudy. "I don't think he saw exactly where I was."

"Let's hope not," said Carlos.

They didn't talk again until they reached the barn. Rudy picked his holdall off the backseat and took it into the barn, followed by Carlos.

Once they were inside, Carlos opened the holdall and shone his torch down into it.

"Excellent work," he said. "We can now move on to the next stage."

They shook hands, before Rudy hurried back outside and sped off into the night.

CHAPTER 18
Microphone Madness

"You may ask why we're here," said Ian Fox.

Nat had got a call early the next morning telling him that the team bus would be picking him up on the coastal road in an hour. He and the other players had been bussed to a large stretch of unattended beach a couple of miles up the coast from Talorca. The sky was light blue, with only a few tiny wisps of cloud. A couple of waterskiers could be seen in the distance.

"To make sandcastles?" shouted Adilson, which got a big laugh.

"Very funny," grinned Fox, "but wrong!"

There were expectant expressions on the players' faces as they waited for their manager to go on.

"Believe it or not, Stan and I have brought you here for a little bit of fun."

"What's fun?" called Emi. Cue more laughs.

"We're going to mix it with some serious training," said Fox. "Last night was a decent result, but we need your performances to step up a gear against our Italian friends from Lazio tomorrow night."

A decent result! Is that the most positive thing the boss can say about us beating Celtic?

"Stan is going to take you through some runs," declared Fox.

Evans called everyone into a bunch and after some stretches he got them jogging on the sand. After this, they did sideways runs and sprints. Everyone was in a good mood and Nat was soon caught up in the atmosphere.

After some two-v-two workouts, in which Nat and Adilson were paired against Emi and Andy Young, Nat excelled in a series of five-a-sides. His session on the beach the other day had been fun, but these games were joyous. He was by far the most experienced squad member at playing beach football and this shone through. His turn of speed, tricks and movement were all excellent, and a couple of times he drew applause from his teammates.

"Have you been playing on Copacabana beach?" enquired Adilson, with a wide grin.

Nat laughed nervously at Adilson's spot-on guess. He would have loved to tell Adilson the truth about his time on Copacabana beach, but this would stand at odds with his official backstory about having lived in America. So he just said, "I wish," and carried on.

The penultimate game was held up when Paulo Carigio and Dean Jobson collided as they both went for the same ball. Being on the same side, one of them should have called for it, but, as was their occasional habit, neither of them did. They were about to have a go at each other but Fox got in between them quickly and was locked into a small 'discussion' with them. It looked a little heated, but a minute later the boss was patting them both on the back, and play restarted.

In the last of the five-a-sides, Nat left the Wildman kicking at air and rounded Graham Dalston with a beautiful twist before thumping the ball home.

"What did you have for breakfast?" asked Stan Evans as the session ended and everyone flopped down onto the sand, taking swigs from the water bottles being handed out.

Nat was pleased about Stan Evans's praise, but as always he wished that Ian Fox would acknowledge him too. Fox did approach him but it wasn't to shower him with praise.

"I saw your old friend Ray Swinton this morning," Fox informed Nat quietly.

"He's not my friend," replied Nat.

"Whatever," went on Fox. "He's out here to cover the tournament for the *Sunday Crest*. Seemed a tiny bit jittery."

Nat frowned.

"I'm sure it's nothing," replied Fox. "Anyway, I thought I'd mention it to you so you're not too surprised when you see him. I'm sure he'll want to interview you along with lots of our players."

"That's OK by me," replied Nat, who, in truth, would be very happy not to see Swinton again for a good while.

After a swim back at the team hotel, Nat hung out in the lobby with Emi. Emi's dad was making progress and there was still no negative news from the tests the hospital was running. They were just about to order a drink when Hatton Rangers's press and PR woman Helen Aldershot approached them. She had short blond hair cut in a bob and round, rosy cheeks.

"Hi guys," she said. "I've just had a request for an interview from a Spanish radio station. They wanted Adilson because his Spanish is pretty good, but he's not around. So they asked if I had a couple of other players who were up for a bit of a laugh and you two came to mind. Would you be interested?"

"Er . . . we don't speak Spanish," said Emi.

"That's not a problem," smiled Aldershot. "The DJ whose show you'd be on has an English mother, so he'd do the interview in English and simultaneously translate it."

"Sounds a bit complicated," said Nat.

"I think they know what they're doing," replied Aldershot. "And it would be good for spreading the Hatton Rangers brand."

"What do you reckon?" asked Emi, glancing at Nat.

Nat thought it over. He wanted to say no, as any contact with the press wasn't a particularly welcome prospect in his position, but he didn't want to appear too defensive.

"Er . . . yeah . . . OK, I suppose" he nodded uncertainly.

"Alright, let's do it," said Emi.

"Great!" beamed Aldershot. "We'll go to the radio station by taxi. Apparently it's only fifteen minutes away."

"When do they want us?" asked Emi.

She checked her watch. "We should leave in half an hour," she replied.

So thirty minutes later, the three of them set off for the radio station, having got the hotel to call a cab. Aldershot sat in the front, Nat and Emi in the back.

"You are footballers?" grinned the driver, looking at Nat and Emi in his rear-view mirror.

They nodded.

"I like Liverpool," he informed them. "Beautiful team, yes?"

"Beautiful," replied Emi, "but not quite as good as us!"

"Your team are OK," said the driver. "Henton Rangers, yes?"

"Hatton Rangers," corrected Aldershot.

It wasn't long before they pulled up in front of a tall, white building, set back from the road and surrounded by a high red brick wall. Aldershot paid the driver, rang the intercom on the front wall and they were buzzed in.

The reception area was all glass and chrome. A man with a bleached Mohican sitting behind a desk made a phone call, and a tall, spindly woman holding a clipboard appeared and asked them to follow her. They walked up a flight of stairs, through the open-plan production area and into a waiting room. They were left there for a few minutes, during which Nat and Emi talked about the next night's Lazio match, with Aldershot dropping her own thoughts into the conversation. She knew more about Lazio than either of them did, so they listened to her description of the keeper Paulo Calari's habit of diving to his left at penalties.

Suddenly the door was flung open and a huge, pot-bellied man with a massive beard and long hair swept into the room. He was wearing a very loud yellow and gold t-shirt and black shorts, with a huge gold medallion round his neck. He was followed in by the wafer-thin woman and a boy who looked no older than ten.

"Hi guys, I'm Paul Rodriguez – the main man of Spanish radio!" he cried flamboyantly. "It's great of you to visit our humble abode!" He waved his arms around, nearly knocking the thin woman over.

He exchanged hearty handshakes with Nat, Emi and Helen.

"This is Claudia, who works as my assistant, and this guy is Marco – my producer," explained Rodriguez.

Nat stared at the ten-year-old-looking man with amazement.

"Claudia's and Marco's English isn't what you'd call first class," chuckled Rodriguez, "so I'll tell you all you need to know. The show goes on air in fifteen minutes and you're our first guests. You'll be on about ten minutes into the show. We'll keep you in the studio for about twenty minutes and then let you out, OK?"

Nat and Emi nodded.

"How are you finding Andalusia?" enquired Rodriguez, taking a giant pear out of his shorts pocket and sinking his teeth into it.

"It's great," replied Emi.

"Very friendly," added Nat.

"You haven't heard me on air yet, have you?" enquired Rodriguez hopefully.

Nat and Emi exchanged a glance.

"Only joking, guys! Make yourselves comfortable and I'll see you in a while."

He exited the room with Claudia and Marco in his wake.

"Wow," said Helen, "he's a bit of a character, isn't he?"

"You could say that," murmured Nat. He was starting to regret agreeing to do the interview. What if Rodriguez started asking questions about Stan Evans discovering him in the States? What if he made some comment about Nat looking too young to play professional football? He could really do without that.

Five minutes later, Claudia came back into the room, smiled awkwardly and motioned for the three of them to follow her. They headed down a corridor and waited outside a door, above which stood a bright red light. When the light went off, Claudia led them inside into the studio. She showed them each to a place around a horseshoe-shaped table covered in green baize, with five microphones on stands. She pointed to headphones on the table and they each put a pair on.

Through a large window they could see Rodriguez and Marco, both wearing headphones, waving encouragingly at them. The red light positioned in the middle of the table stayed off for a further few seconds and then lit up. The show was live on air again. Through the headphones Nat heard Paul talking fast in Spanish, but a few seconds later, the DJ switched to English, alternating with a Spanish translation.

"Emi Adeyo and Nat Dixon are footballers from the English Premier League side Hatton Rangers, and guess what? They're here in my studio right now! How about that! I issue you both the warmest welcome to Spain, gentlemen! You're here for the six-team tournament hosted by our beloved local team – Talorca FC. How are you finding our little corner of this great nation?"

Rodriguez quickly translated into Spanish.

"So far, so good," replied Emi.

"Good facilities, great organisation," Nat chipped in.

"Tell us what it's like to play in the English Premier League," said Rodriguez. "We see loads of games on TV and we LOVE IT!"

"It's very competitive," answered Nat.

"We have plenty of Spanish players based in England," cut in Rogriguez. "It often takes them a few months to acclimatise to the English style of playing."

"That's right," nodded Emi. "Your teams out here *can* play very fast, but they sweep the ball around in a much more relaxed way. There's more time on the ball. Back home it's receive, control and pass."

"You beat Celtic one-nil last night – a quite magnificent victory, with your Brazilian star Adilson scoring the winning goal. How are you feeling about tomorrow night's Lazio game? Will they be tougher opponents than Celtic?"

"No disrespect to Celtic, but I think Lazio will be a harder game," responded Emi. "They have some excellent players and they're very experienced at playing European games. We'll have to be on top form to get something out of the match."

"Nat, we read something about you and the ex-Hatton Rangers goalkeeper Chris Webb. He was involved in a match-fixing scam that you helped stop. Can you tell us exactly what happened?"

Helen Aldershot shook her head forcefully.

"Er . . . I can't say anything about it," answered Nat. "There's a court case to come."

"OK," nodded Rodriguez. "We're going to a break, but stay tuned because these two great players are going to be hanging around for a bit longer and we have a beautiful surprise lined up for them!"

The red light went off while a Spanish car advert played.

"What's the surprise?" asked Aldershot nervously into Emi's microphone.

"Don't worry," grinned Rodriguez from the other side of the glass, "it'll be fun."

Aldershot looked anxiously at Nat and Emi. "Any ideas?" she whispered.

They both shrugged their shoulders.

Next up was an advert for a fizzy orange drink, followed by one for a bank. During the bank advert the studio door was pushed open by Claudia and in stepped . . . Alberto Tieras.

Nat, Emi and Helen Aldershot looked up at the giant Talorca defender in shock. He really was massive – six foot five, with a huge, puffed out chest, straggly, light brown hair and two sneering eyes sunk deep into his face. Before they could say anything, he slipped into a chair on the opposite side of the studio table and pulled on a pair of headphones. A second later the red light flashed on.

"OK, boys and girls!" crowed Rodriguez. "We have something very special now for you. Alongside our friends from the English Premier League, we have our very own Talorca legend and club captain, Mr Alberto Tieras."

There was whooping from the control room and Rodriguez held a quick chat in Spanish with Tieras before switching back to English.

"So, Alberto, what do you have to say to our English buddies?"

"I wish them luck in their match against Lazio tomorrow night," replied Tieras slowly in English.

"Will you be giving them the same message if they win their group, Talorca win theirs and your two teams meet in the final?"

"No!" laughed Tieras. "If the final is them against us, then they become our enemies."

Helen Aldershot frowned.

"We don't really see it like that," said Emi quickly.

"That does not surprise me," laughed Tieras. "In England players are treated like princesses. Things are different here. We are treated like men so we behave like men. We fight when we need too."

Nat quickly glanced at his companions. Helen Aldershot was sitting with her mouth open so wide it looked like a basketball could fit inside it. Emi was shaking his head and looking angry.

"We see it as a game, not a war," said Nat testily.

"Say what you want," sneered Tieras with contempt. "Talorca are the only real team in this battle . . . in this war. We won't be giving respect to an English team that finished . . . where was it. . .? Seventeenth out of a league of twenty!"

"Hang on a second," cut in Emi, glaring at the Talorca captain. "We're not here for a war! We're here for a friendly tournament, hosted by your club!"

"Rubbish!" cried Tieras. "Every football match is a war. You should take that to heart. It might help you next season. Maybe you could finish sixteenth! How about that?"

"That's it!" snapped Emi, standing up, throwing his headphones onto the table and storming towards the door. Nat and Aldershot quickly got to their feet and followed him. Tieras roared with gleeful laughter.

"Hang on a second!" cried Rodriguez stepping out of the control room. "It was only a bit of fun!"

"You set us up!" shouted Emi.

"You're totally out of order!" added Nat.

"Guys, come on!" pleaded Rodriguez. "Don't take it like that!"

But they brushed past him and took the stairs at a pace. Marching back out into the sun, Aldershot flagged down a taxi. She looked very pale and distressed.

"I am SO sorry," she said hoarsely. "I had no idea anything like that would happen."

"It's not your fault," replied Emi. "They obviously had the whole thing planned – you know, let's wind up those lightweight English visitors!"

"Tieras is just a macho idiot," said Nat angrily. "Most Spanish fans are nothing like that. They love the Premier League and respect the players."

"Absolutely!" nodded Aldershot. "He was well out of line."

"And he clearly doesn't watch any of our games," added Emi. "I'd love to know what the Wildman would think of his outburst."

"Look," said Nat with a deep sigh. "Let's just get back to the hotel and chill. It's only some small radio station – chances are no one heard it."

But as they flagged down another taxi, all three of them felt hot, flustered and very angry.

CHAPTER 19
Hire It

Carlos and Rudy pulled up in front of the newly-built office block, its white stone walls glistening in the sun. Carlos was wearing a blue baseball cap, dark sunglasses and a suit. The photo accompanying the story about his prison escape in the paper was old and grainy, but he wanted to be absolutely sure that no one recognised him. Rudy was also wearing a suit, but his sunglasses were resting on top of his head. The man from the property management company was standing by the front door of the complex. He was wearing a pinstriped suit and narrow glasses and was on his mobile. The minute he saw Carlos and Rudy, he ended his call and walked over to greet them.

"Vladimir Daskov," he declared, by way of introduction. In spite of his Russian roots, his Spanish was perfect and almost accent-free. "You said on the phone you're interested in renting out one of the spaces here?"

"Yes," nodded Carlos, shaking Daskov's hand. "We've heard that the entire place is still unoccupied?"

"At present, yes," nodded Daskov, swiping a card on a

panel by the front entrance. The door opened inwards and they followed him through. "We've had plenty of interest, though. It's a prime location with excellent local amenities and is proving to be very popular. I would strongly suggest that, if you're interested, you put down a deposit today."

Carlos and Rudy ignored this opening salvo of sales patter and followed Daskov to the third and top floor.

"Each floor has four units," Daskov announced, turning two keys in the last door on their left and pushing it open.

The three of them stepped into a small entranceway, which opened out to a large, empty square. At the far side were two large windows. There was a door on the far right.

"When do you envisage other tenants arriving?" asked Carlos casually.

"I can't give you an exact date," replied Daskov, "but as I said, it's popular and I'm showing several units to other interested parties over the next few days. Obviously, if you put down a deposit for this one, it's yours and I won't show it to anyone else."

"Sounds reasonable," nodded Rudy.

"Might I ask what line of business you're in?" enquired Daskov.

"Of course," said Carlos. "We're in website construction and maintenance."

"Really?" replied Daskov. "Our company website has had all sorts of problems recently and we're not satisfied with the team maintaining it. Would you be willing to take a look at it?"

Carlos and Rudy exchanged a glance.

"Er . . . that won't be possible at the minute, because of our packed schedule," replied Rudy, "but give us a few weeks and we'll see what we can do."

"Do you have a business card?"

"Sorry, I gave the last one out yesterday," answered Carlos. "But as soon as we have new ones, we'll get one to you."

Daskov stared at them for a few seconds and then walked over to the windows. They joined him and looked out at the long green field that ran behind the complex.

"If you fancy a bit of sunbathing, you have access to the roof, which is surrounded by a safety fence and is open to all tenants," said Daskov. "Although I assume you'll be too busy with your website designs."

Was there a trace of suspicion in his voice?

"Thanks for that," smiled Carlos.

Daskov then opened the door on the right hand side of the unit and showed his prospective tenants a small toilet-washroom, which possessed brand new, gleaming fittings and an air vent.

"So, what do you think, gentlemen?" said Daskov, wrapping up his pitch. "You won't find many spaces like this at such a reasonable rate in the whole of Andalusia. You're welcome to go away and think about it, but if I were you, and you like it, I'd grab it pretty quick!"

Before he'd even finished speaking, Rudy was reaching into his jacket pocket and pulling out a large bundle of notes. Daskov's eyes lit up when the money appeared. It was rare for tenants to make such instant decisions but obviously his patter had done the trick.

"This is the deposit and this is for the first month's rent," said Rudy, counting out some notes and handing them over. Carlos had made more money in prison than he'd ever made outside it. He'd delivered parcels to various inmates, who had arranged for him to be paid handsomely in return for keeping his mouth shut. "After that, we'll set up a direct debit and pay monthly, if that's OK?"

"Perfect!" beamed Daskov who had rarely closed a sale so speedily. "Delighted to have you on board!" He took the notes, checked they constituted the correct amount and folded them into his inside jacket pocket. "I'll need to see a couple of references from past landlords," he said. No sooner were the words out of his mouth than Rudy was presenting him with two immaculate references on official paper.

"May I keep these?" asked Daskov, quickly scanning them approvingly.

"Absolutely," replied Rudy.

"There are some documents I need you to sign."

Daskov reached into his briefcase and extracted a small sheaf of papers. As there were no work surfaces to lean on, he pressed his briefcase against the wall, placed a document against it and handed Carlos a pen. Carlos flicked through the document, then signed and dated it in the right places – with every detail he entered being completely false. Daskov took the completed document then handed Carlos a second one. He filled this in just like the first.

"Excellent," said Daskov, retrieving his briefcase and slipping both documents inside. "When would you like to move in?"

"Now," replied Carlos.

Daskov looked a little surprised. Normally clients gave themselves at least a few days to get everything up and ready. "Do you have much to bring in?" he asked. "We have a good deal with a removals company."

"We're fine," responded Rudy, "but thanks for the offer."

"OK," said Daskov. "Good to do business with you."

"Likewise," said Carlos.

Daskov reached into his pocket and handed them two pass cards for the front entrance and two sets of keys for the unit.

"Any problems, just give me a call," he said, opening the front door and standing on the threshold of the unit.

"Thank you," said Carlos, before he and Rudy shook hands with Daskov a final time.

"I wish you all the best," smiled Daskov, before he hurried downstairs and out of the complex. He crossed the road and got into his low, blue, sporty car. As he drove away, his joy at getting these new tenants was tempered with a twinge of unease. There was something slightly odd about these two guys. He couldn't put his finger on it, but it was definitely there.

But then he remembered the notes in his jacket pocket and decided that they were probably fine – they both looked respectable, their references were excellent, they'd paid *in cash, and it had sounded like they were going to take the unit on for a decent period of time. Having reassured himself, he turned on the radio and put his foot down.*

CHAPTER 20
The Deal on Offer

"Why on earth did you do it?" shouted a red-faced Ian Fox, who was waiting in the hotel lobby for the returning radio station troupe.

"What do you mean?" asked a perturbed Helen Aldershot. "You heard it?"

"Of course I heard it!" thundered Fox. "The bloody thing's gone viral! I've already had some English journalists on the phone wanting a quote from me about my response to it!"

Aldershot's face looked as though it was going to crumple inwards like a paper bag. "It's all my fault," she said, going very red. "When I spoke to them, it sounded really genuine and. . ."

"I'm not interested in what it sounded like *before* the interview," snapped Fox. "I'm more concerned about how two of my players were verbally abused by the captain of the team that's hosting this tournament."

"It wasn't Helen's fault," said Nat firmly. "There was no way she could have known we were being set up. When we got there everything seemed in order. They just sprang it on us."

Aldershot smiled gratefully at Nat.

"Nat's right!" nodded Emi. "No one's at fault here. Anyway, it's no big deal."

"Of course it's a big deal!" cried Fox. "I will NOT have my players attacked or ridiculed on air – even if it is on some local radio station. Do you get me?"

Nat suddenly felt as if the three of them were naughty school kids who'd just been caught skiving.

"Alright," huffed Fox, "but no more interviews, Helen, unless they're authorised by me."

"Of course," agreed Aldershot.

"Good," replied Fox. "I'll see you all later on the bus to the stadium. We're leaving at four thirty."

* * *

Ray Swinton was sitting by his hotel pool in a dark mood. There had been no word from the police about the stolen notebooks – nothing. Part of him was hoping they'd be found dropped in a local street, and for this reason there was one vital phone call he hadn't yet made.

He took an angry slug from a bottle of water and clenched his fists in frustration. Those notebooks contained thousands of phone numbers, notes and lines of enquiry that would be impossible to replace in full. He'd told himself over and over again that the most important information was backed up on his laptop, and this he never let out of his sight. But there were plenty of other things that had been recorded solely in the notebooks.

He was taking a bite of a cracker when his mobile went. Maybe it was the police saying they'd found his things.

"Ray Swinton," he answered.

"Ray Swinton from the *Sunday Crest?*" enquired a voice with an Eastern European accent.

"Yes, that's me."

"I have something that is important to you."

Swinton felt a judder in his chest. "What do you mean?"

"There was a robbery at your hotel a couple of days ago, yes?"

"How do you know about that?"

"I have your notebooks."

"You broke into my hotel room!" hissed Swinton furiously.

"Not me," responded the voice. "My . . . colleagues."

"Well you and your colleagues can go to hell!" snarled Swinton menacingly. "I want those notebooks back NOW!"

He looked up and saw that several people round the pool were staring at him.

"Give them back to me!" he hissed, lowering his voice.

"If only it were that simple," replied the voice. "I have to confess that finding your notebooks was a lucky bi-product of our little break-in. But now we have them I can see that they contain some very interesting material. If you want them back, you will have to pay for them."

"You've got to be joking!"

"I don't joke Mr Swinton – I am a businessman."

"No you're not!" snarled Swinton. "You're a blackmailer. And anyway, they're not worth anything!"

"Then why are you getting so worked up about them?"

Swinton's mind whirred with frenzied activity. There was definitely some very juicy information in the notebooks. Much of it was scribbled in his own spidery hand, which very few people could decipher. On the other hand, if anyone did manage to make sense of it and handed it to a rival newspaper, that would be disastrous.

"How much do you want?" he asked.

"£30,000."

Swinton let out a horrified laugh. "£30,000!" he hissed in disbelief. "Are you out of your mind? You can forget about any deal if that's the sort of sum we're talking about!"

"Fine," replied the caller smoothly. "£20,000."

"No way!" snarled Swinton.

"OK," said the caller, a slight note of tension entering his voice. "£15,000, but that's my final offer."

"Again no!"

"If that's the way you want it, I will start passing the information from the notebooks to other newspapers."

Swinton felt a surge of white-hot fury. The man had read his mind. He couldn't let that happen!

"You are running out of time, Mr Swinton," said the caller. "I have said that £15,000 is my final offer. If you cannot meet that, then I'm afraid the notebooks will be sold on."

Swinton wiped the palm of his hand over his mouth and cheeks. Hundreds of thoughts and possibilities flashed through his brain as he tried to calculate the best position to take.

"Mr Swinton?" demanded the voice.

Swinton cleared his throat. "I'll pay you £10,000 and that's it. You hand me the notebooks, I pay you the cash. And you show the material to no one else, got it?"

There was a pause on the line. "You have a deal," said the caller.

Swinton breathed a small sigh of relief, though where he was going to get ten grand from was beyond him at that moment.

"Now we have agreed the price, you will listen to these instructions very carefully," said the caller.

Swinton grabbed a pen and a piece of paper.

"You will go to the central bus station in Talorca on Friday night. Near the centre of the station is the stop for the number twenty-eight bus to Málaga. You will arrive at the stop at 7.30 p.m. sharp.

"I will approach you. You will not approach me. You will have the cash in one medium-sized envelope."

Swinton gulped at the thought of going into a bank and asking for a sum like that, but he carried on writing.

"You will hand the envelope to me, and I will pass you the notebooks."

"Do you want me to bring flowers?" asked Swinton sourly.

"This is no time for bad jokes," said the caller, with irritation. "Don't contact the police about this phone call and don't bring any police officers with you. Even if they are in civilian clothes I will spot them immediately and the deal will be off. And you will tell no one else about this deal."

"I get the message," snapped Swinton.

"Remember, Mr Swinton. 7.30 p.m. at the number twenty-eight bus stop. If you are late, the deal is off."

"OK!" seethed Swinton. "And there's one thing I want to say to you. If you fail to hand over the notebooks as soon as I give you the cash, you won't leave the bus station with any bones intact. Do you understand *that*?"

But the caller had signed off, like a sharp slap in the face.

CHAPTER 21
News Shock

Back at Inés's place, José's door was open a fraction again and Nat found himself looking through the gap. José wasn't there, but on his bed was a pile of car manuals. Nat checked the corridor behind him was empty and quickly dipped into the room. The manuals were concerned with top end cars – Porsches and Lamborghinis. As Nat stared, a thought suddenly hit him.

He'd seen José holding a large wad of cash the other day and had no idea how he'd come by it. Well, maybe this was the answer – maybe José was involved in some type of car theft racket, an industry that turned over millions of pounds every year. Inés certainly didn't have that kind of cash and as José wasn't officially working, there was no job to pull in that kind of wage. So maybe this could be the way it all fitted together.

Nat stepped out of José's room and walked back to his own, thinking about the whirlwind of events that had taken place just a short while back – the Chris Webb and Tanner plot and his role in stopping it. If José was involved in stealing cars, while Nat didn't exactly approve, he wasn't going to get involved. He'd experienced more than his fair share of drama in recent weeks and he didn't want an ounce more.

He'd just sat down on the bed when his phone went. He expected it to be his dad. But it wasn't.

"Nat, it's Ray Swinton."

Nat felt his whole body tense. "What do you want, Mr Swinton?"

"There's something we need to discuss."

"If it's about the Lazio game, can we do it tomorrow?" replied Nat in a guarded voice.

"It's not about the Lazio game."

"Well, what is it?"

"We have a problem," sighed Swinton.

"What do you mean?"

"There was a break-in at my hotel and some of my notebooks were taken."

"I'm sorry to hear that," said Nat, "but what's that got to do with me?"

Swinton took a deep breath and blew out his cheeks. "One of the notebooks has some notes about my suspicions concerning your age. My handwriting is pretty illegible, but if anyone put their mind to it they could see some thoughts and jottings about the possibility of you being under sixteen."

"Oh my God!" exclaimed Nat in horror, his back

straightening with shock. "Please tell me you're making this up?"

"I'm sorry, Nat, but I'm telling you the truth."

"Why did you leave your notebooks in your room if they contain vital stuff?" demanded Nat angrily.

"I thought they were only vital to me."

"But now they're out there, right?"

"Look, Nat, there's no easy way to say this. I had a call from a guy who said that he has them."

"This just gets worse!" gulped Nat.

"The guy demanded money to get them back. He said if I don't pay he'll show them to other papers. After an argument we agreed on a price. I'm meeting him on Friday night for the handover."

"So you'll be taking the police with you?"

"No," said Swinton flatly. "He says if I bring the police I'll never see the notebooks again."

"How much money does he want?"

"It doesn't matter."

Nat mentally switched out of the call for a few moments, trying to get things straight. The notebooks had been stolen but Swinton's handwriting was terrible. Was it so bad that someone else wouldn't be able to read it, or was it decipherable with a bit of time and effort? If someone at another paper got wind of the underage story, Nat could be heading for massive trouble.

"I want to talk something over with you," Swinton went on.

Nat shook his head. *I can't believe this is happening!*

"Alright, you've got ten minutes," he replied, lying down on his bed and feeling as if the wheels were really coming off the juggernaut of his football career. Swinton outlined a possible way of dealing with the thief and Nat listened in stony silence.

No sooner had he finished speaking to Swinton than there was a knock on his door and Inés poked her head round it. "Could I have a word in the kitchen, Nat?"

Nat gazed at her blankly. Suddenly everyone wanted to speak to him. "Sure," he nodded, "I'll be there in a minute."

When he got to the kitchen, Inés was sitting at the table staring out of the window.

"Er . . . are you OK?" asked Nat.

Inés looked up quickly and forced a smile. "I'm fine," she replied. "Please, take a seat."

He sat down and she poured him a glass of lemonade.

"It's about José," she said.

Is this going to be more about the accident?

"You seem like a nice boy. I know you're only sixteen but you come across as much older. And I know I shouldn't burden you, but sometimes it's very hard not to talk about the things that matter the most."

Nat's mouth opened and shut.

"I'm very worried about him," she went on. "He's only a year older than you, but look at the difference in your situations. You have a whole life to look forward

156

to, potentially a good career, a stable set-up. He has . . . nothing."

"Because of the accident?"

Inés nodded. "As I've told you, the crash robbed him of two things – his father and his career. How is he going to find anything else that even comes close to football? How is he ever going to make a hundredth of the money he'd have earned as a professional player?"

Nat's mind instantly locked on the bundle of notes and the top-of-the-range car manuals he'd seen on José's bed. Clearly Inés knew nothing about any of it. Maybe that's what happened to some of the footballers who didn't make it – maybe some of them turned to crime because it was the only way they'd earn comparable money.

"And he's so angry all of the time," said Inés. "He used to be a very relaxed sort of boy, but now you can see constant anger in his face."

"Was he very close to your husband?"

"Incredibly close," sighed Inés.

Nat knew that feeling all too well. "Was José's injury so bad that they instantly knew he'd never play football again?" he asked.

"The diagnosis was pretty quick, yes," she nodded. "They didn't tell him for a few days at my request – he was trying to come to terms with the loss of his father. It was a terrible time. When they finally explained the situation to him, instead of screaming and crying, he went into his shell – he clammed up and said nothing for over a week. It was very distressing."

"Has José talked about any other potential careers he could follow?"

"No. But he loved cars when he was younger. I'm hoping he might go back to that – be a mechanic, something like that."

Maybe Nat was way off-beam with his car-theft theory. José might just be exploring a career as a mechanic. It didn't explain the big pile of cash, though.

"But I can't talk to him," Inés went on. "He's so inward-looking, and if ever I try to make a suggestion, he gets angry and tells me to leave him alone."

"Maybe he just needs more time," suggested Nat.

"Of course," nodded Inés, "but how long? Another year? Another two years? It feels like he's wasting his life. Yes, he's still young, but time passes quickly and I don't want him to look back and realise there was a huge hole in his life for ten years."

Nat was about to reply, when the kitchen door flew open and a furious José stormed in. His cheeks were scarlet and his eyes large and glaring. He yelled furiously at his mother in Spanish. She stood up and shouted back at him. He took a couple of steps forward and smashed his fist down on the kitchen table, bellowing at her again, this time for longer. But before she could answer him, he turned and stamped out of the room, slamming the door behind him.

Inés said nothing for at least a minute, but when she

did, it was in a very quiet, low voice. "He is angry with me for talking to you about him."

"I'm sorry," said Nat, standing up. "I . . . er . . . I guess I'll go and grab a shower."

Inés nodded wearily. "Thank you for listening," she said.

"No problem," replied Nat, but he didn't see how listening to her for five minutes could alleviate the problem even the tiniest bit. It was a bleak scenario and whichever way you looked at it, it felt like José was in trouble.

CHAPTER 22
Lazio Loom

"Hey Emi!"

Nat ran over to his friend, who was signing an autograph for a Spanish boy outside the El Mar Stadium. It was just after 9.30 a.m. and the sun was already heating the metal shutters at the front of the stadium's box office. Emi finished signing and shook hands with the child, who ran back to his friends, waving his piece of paper in the air as if it were a valuable artefact from the *Titanic*.

Thoughts of Ray Swinton's missing notebooks had been flooding Nat's mind, but he knew that if he kept thinking about them it would seriously affect his performances on the pitch. For the time being, he had to place them to one side and focus on the team and his fellow players.

"Nat, how's it going?" said Emi.

"How's your dad doing?"

"Thanks for asking again," replied Emi with a smile. "He came out of hospital last night and he's back home. He'll have to go back for some more tests next week but the doctor think he's going to be fine."

"That's brilliant," said Nat, putting an arm round Emi's shoulder.

"You two – let's get going, we have a big match tonight, remember?" It was Stan Evans calling over to them and tapping his watch.

On the El Mar pitch, the atmosphere was less jokey than the other days. Fox encouraged this. His expression was solemn.

"I don't need to tell you, lads, that if we win or draw tonight against Lazio, we make it into Saturday's final. If we lose, we'll be flying home tomorrow morning. I'm well aware that Lazio are a top Serie A team, with many seasons of European Champions League experience behind them, and that we are a team very new to the heady world of the Premier League. But none of that matters tonight."

The manager swivelled his head round, making eye contact with every one of his players.

"Defenders – you're facing a potentially rough ride tonight. Their two strikers Laurent Breton and Luigi Fellini scored fifty-four goals between them last season. They're fast, tricky and neither of them are afraid to shoot from distance. Having said all that, they both get frustrated when they don't get good service."

"What about midfield?" asked Dean Jobson, with a quick and not-very-friendly sideways glance at Paulo Carigio.

"Dean, you'll be sitting in front of the back four.

Paulo will be taking the more attacking role tonight."

Carigio nodded. Jobson's top lip curled unhappily.

"Sorry, Dean, but that's where I want you and that's where you'll play – unless of course you want to warm up the subs bench?"

"No thanks, boss," replied Jobson.

"I didn't think so," nodded Fox.

It crossed Nat's mind that the gaffer should drop Jobson for this game and put Jermaine Clifton on instead. Wouldn't Jobson be out there eyeing each of Carigio's attacking runs with envy? Maybe it really was time to accept that they couldn't play together?

"I'm not going to wait until two hours before the match to tell you the team this time, I'm going to tell you *now*," continued Fox. "Adilson, you'll be on the left flank, Jermaine you're starting on the right."

Jermaine Clifton nodded, but Pierre Sacrois's face was darkened by a frown. This was the first time in six months he hadn't been in a Hatton Rangers starting eleven.

"Dennis and Robbie, you'll start in attack again."

Nat felt a pang in his stomach, but in reality he hadn't expected anything different, even though he'd done pretty well against Celtic. He knew that having unrealistic expectations was a waste of time.

"The game plan for tonight is to go at them. They won't be expecting us to play an attacking game, but that's exactly what we're going to do. If we sit back and play like the away team, inviting them to come at us, they'll cut us in ribbons. We push them on the flanks and through the centre. While I don't want you to go all Lionel Messi on me, Adilson, I do want you to play a pretty free role."

"Yes, boss," nodded Adilson seriously.

"We think they have two weak links. The first is in central defence with Carlunos. He has a massive reputation but we're not sure he fully deserves it. At set pieces he sometimes takes his eye off the ball because he's concentrating so hard on pushing attackers around. The team conceded at least five or six goals last season directly because of this. The second is at left-back – Roger Salba had a bit of a bad patch at the end of the Italian season. It looked like his confidence left him. So have a go at him – shake the tree and see if the fruit falls."

In the training session, Nat stuck to the high standards he'd set himself after the first day's poor start. He was mindful of the gaffer's words about breaking up Lazio attacks quickly, and he ran, chased and harried. At the end of the first half of the session, the starting eleven went through some moves against the remaining seven and Nat managed to get in a perfectly-timed sliding tackle on Paulo Carigio and to steal the ball from Adilson with a strong challenge. The Brazilian went down but got up quickly and slapped Nat's palm. Stan Evans nodded his approval at Nat.

Just give me a chance, Mr Evans! Put in a good word for me with the boss!

Dean Jobson hung back as Ian Fox had ordered, though

you could see the dismay on his face when Paulo Carigio swapped a one-two with Jermaine Clifton and smashed the ball home past Jack Bell.

Nat and Emi stayed out on the pitch when the others had gone in, with Nat running at his friend. Emi didn't hold back on his tackles, but a couple of times Nat skinned him. Emi wasn't best pleased by this, but he had to acknowledge Nat's speed and movement. When they were finished, they sat down on the grass for a breather.

"What do you think of the gaffer giving Dean the defensive role tonight?" asked Nat.

"Disaster," huffed Emi with concern. "Can you really see him hanging back while Paulo is hurtling up the pitch? If it was up to me I'd definitely drop one of them, probably Dean."

"Me too," nodded Nat.

"But that's Fox for you," said Emi. "He has his set ideas and thinks that by sheer force of personality he can take everyone with him. And he's wrong on something else too."

"Go on," said Nat.

"You've been playing far better than Robbie and you should start," said Emi. "I'm not just saying that because we're mates. You're fitter than him, you're faster than him and your finishing's way above his at the minute."

"You reckon?"

"I know," grinned Emi, "but I can see it from the boss's point of view. Robbie's much more experienced than you and it would be hard for Fox to drop him. But if we want to beat Lazio we'd be in a much better position with you out there rather than Robbie."

Nat felt a shot of pride. In his heart of hearts, he knew he'd been playing a notch above Robbie Clarke, but it would have sounded arrogant coming from him; Emi saying it, however, was a great confidence booster.

CHAPTER 23
A Possible Spy

"Pass me the big box," said Carlos, looking up from the table when Rudy entered the unit. There were two boxes on the floor. Rudy picked up the larger one and walked over to Carlos with it. They'd dropped off the boxes, tables, chairs and a large holdall of equipment first thing that morning.

"I've got some news," said Rudy.

"What kind of news?"

"I just saw Daskov. He was showing the space at the other end of this floor to a big bald guy."

Carlos frowned.

"They were just inside the front door so I hung back and listened," said Rudy. "The guy said he wanted to take it now. I heard Daskov counting off the notes. Don't you think it's a bit weird that someone's taken it so soon after we took this one and is also paying in cash?"

"Maybe the bald guy just phoned him this morning," suggested Carlos.

"Maybe," said Rudy, walking over to the window and looking out across the field. "But what happens if it's not like that? What happens if it's connected to your break-out?"

"What – you think the bald guy is a cop and he's staking us out?"

"Could be," answered Rudy nervously. "He might be taking the unit to spy on us and make sure it's you."

"There's no way they'll have traced us here," said Carlos calmly. "I haven't been seen in public and Daskov doesn't know who I am."

"What if he does?" said Rudy urgently. "What if he did recognise you and immediately informed the police? If that's what happened, we're in big trouble."

"You've been watching too many crime movies," smiled Carlos reassuringly. "We're safe here. The bald guy and Daskov and anyone else who may rent a unit here haven't got a clue what we're doing. If we keep ourselves to ourselves we'll be fine, OK?"

"I don't like it," muttered Rudy.

"Well, get over it," ordered Carlos, his voice suddenly commanding. "Until anyone knocks on the door brandishing handcuffs we're safe. Now pass me the small box and let's get on with it."

Rudy stepped away from the window and went to pick up the other box. Carlos's words made sense but Rudy was still on edge – it would only take one snooper and they'd be blown out of the water. He'd keep a close eye on the bald man so that if anything were afoot he'd be the first to know.

He handed the second box to Carlos and they pressed on.

CHAPTER 24
Crunch Time

As the Hatton Rangers team bus drove past the front of the stadium, Nat, Emi and Kelvin looked out of the window.

"Check out how many Lazio fans there are!" exclaimed Emi.

He was right. There'd been plenty of them at the Lazio v Celtic game, but their numbers had massively swelled for this one.

Nat and the others had spent the afternoon at the team hotel, Nat trying not to think about Swinton's lost notebooks and to focus on the game.

"Don't worry about it," called Stan Evans, who was checking out the Lazio fans too. "Our supporters will be fantastic. They'll give as good as they get. All you lot have to do is win the game!"

"It's as easy as that, is it?" shouted Emi.

"Absolutely!" replied Evans.

The coach left the main road, turned left down a narrow side road and pulled into the players' car park.

168

Several officials from El Mar were there to greet the Rangers squad and led them into the building.

"Same changing room as before!" shouted Andy Young, who was easily the most superstitious member of the squad. "It's a good omen!"

"OK, listen in, everyone!" shouted Stan Evans. "The gaffer has a thing or two to say."

All eyes switched to Fox. "I've already told you how important this game is and we've talked about our tactics. Dean, I know you're not enamoured by your defensive role but I need you to be there for us tonight – I'm relying on you."

Jobson nodded at the boss, but Nat saw the hangdog look of dejection that Jobson couldn't quite remove from his face.

"As I said in training, we attack. There's no point in just defending."

"Press them," chipped in the Wildman, "and we'll score."

With twenty minutes to go before kick off, Stan Evans led the players onto the pitch for some stretches and runs. The stadium was already buzzing with excitement. Nat lined up with Jensen, Clarke and Sinclair, taking shots against Graham Dalston. He got a couple of sweet strikes in the net. Then it was back inside. The first eleven got changed and the two teams filed out onto the pitch to great applause and some boos – although who these were for wasn't clear. The Wildman had won the toss earlier in the evening so Hatton Rangers got to play in their home strip – white and green vertical stripes, white shorts and green socks. Lazio wore their second away kit of dark blue shirts, blue shorts and half blue, half black socks.

Nat took up his place on the bench next to a very sour-looking Pierre Sacrois, who was still livid about not making the starting eleven. He was muttering under his breath in French. Nat caught Ian Fox's name a couple of times.

In the middle of the field, doing runs and stretches by himself, was genius playmaker Arturo Tassi, who had so impressed against Celtic.

Tassi is already a big player, but there's no question – he's going to be huge.

The first ten minutes of the game went brilliantly for Rangers. Adilson was all over the place, dragging defenders out of position and spraying balls to Jensen and Clarke. They both managed decent shots and this put the Lazio defence on a rather startled, high-alert footing. Lazio's Tassi hardly touched the ball.

Then, on fourteen minutes, Rangers – or, more specifically, Dean Jobson – messed up. He had just received a pass from left-back Andy Young, but instead of threading it across to Jermaine Clifton, he hesitated, and Laurent Breton stole it from him. Lazio broke at breakneck pace, Breton's exquisite pass splitting the Rangers back four, who weren't expecting Jobson's error. Tassi ran onto the pass and charged towards the Rangers goal. The Wildman sprang forward to try and prise the ball off him, but Tassi quickly squared it to Luigi Fellini, who smashed a curling shot into the bottom right-hand corner of Dalston's goal.

The Lazio players mobbed Fellini and Tassi.

"NO!" yelled Fox.

Jobson looked distraught.

"Head up, Dean!" screamed Fox. "Press up and hit them back!"

For a while, Rangers did exactly this – running at the Lazio defence and mopping up at the back to ensure they didn't concede again. Dennis Jensen went on an excellent run, but he was forced out towards the left corner flag. In the battle to escape the attentions of two Lazio defenders, he took a knock on his right calf muscle and went down. The Rangers physiotherapist Colin Dempsey jumped up from the bench, grabbed his bag and ran over to Jensen. With his help, Jensen stood, but he only managed to limp across to the touchline. Nat's heart rose up in expectation, but a spray from one of Dempsey's healing canisters eased the pain, and thirty seconds later the referee waved Jensen back on.

It looked like Rangers would go in at half-time one-nil down, but three minutes before the forty-five were up, Lazio struck again. Tassi went on a mesmerising run that left several Rangers players in his wake. When he burst into the penalty area, Emi and Kelvin rushed in to block him, but he lifted the ball over them both, ran onto it and volleyed home with a wonder strike. It was an absolutely supreme goal, but unfortunately it went to the wrong team.

Tassi was pounced on by his teammates, while Ian Fox jumped up and down at the edge of the technical area, like a toddler who's just been told he can't have the last piece of chocolate.

"Why didn't anyone pick Tassi up?" he shrieked in rage.

Soon after, the referee blew for half-time. The Rangers manager was off down the tunnel in a blur of speed. Nat knew Fox's half-time talk would be brutal, but it was even worse than he'd imagined.

"That performance was a bloody disgrace!" he shouted, when everyone had congregated back in the changing room. "Dean – I don't know what the HELL you were doing when you gave the ball away for the first goal. I just don't get it. Lazio must have thought it was all of their birthdays, bank holidays and Christmases come at the same time! It was a gift! And you're *all* to blame for the second goal. Talk about ball-watching! We know Tassi can run and score, so what did you do? You gave him acres of space! Unbelievable!"

"You're right, boss – it was rubbish," nodded the Wildman. "But we all take responsibility for *both* goals."

Dean Jobson gave the Wildman a grateful nod.

"OK, let's put the first half to bed" said Fox, easing the anger out of his voice. "We need a new game plan for the second half, because I cannot stand another forty-five minutes like that. We're two-nil down. As long as we don't concede again, we can get back into it. There's no point in just defending, we have to score, so from now on, Dean, you can forget about your defensive responsibilities and join up with Carigio to support the forwards."

Jobson smiled in relief.

And then Fox sprang a surprise. "Dennis I'm taking you off. You took a nasty knock on your calf – I don't want to make it any worse."

"It's nothing, boss," insisted Jensen. "Colin said it's fine. Honestly, I can't feel it. I'm fine."

"Decision's already made," replied Fox firmly. "Nat you're on."

No way – I'm on for the whole second half!

Although Dennis Jensen was clearly crushed, he gave Nat a positive smile.

"Nat, you and Robbie are charged with dragging us back into the game by getting the ball into the back of the net, supported by Adilson and Jermaine, with Jobson and Carigio backing you up. Think of it as a six-man attack where we're taking the game to them, and pray they don't catch us on the break early in the half. Let's make life seriously uncomfortable for them in the next forty-five minutes."

"Remember, lads, a draw will put us into Saturday's final!" cried the Wildman. "We CAN do it!"

Nat and the rest of the team shouted their support.

So when Nat moved back down the tunnel he was in his Rangers kit, and instead of heading for the subs' bench, he strode to the centre circle with Robbie Clarke. He jumped up and down several times, heading the air.

"I'm not ready to go home," said Robbie.

"Me neither," nodded Nat.

From the whistle, Rangers attacked, and Nat was right in the thick of things. In the fiftieth minute, he released Adilson, who took a quick shot that went just over the bar.

Jermaine Clifton then had a half-chance that he scuffed. In the sixty-first minute, Nat received a pass from Emi in the centre circle. He looked up and saw Clarke just up ahead and they swapped passes. Nat was now approaching the penalty area and switched play out to the left, where Adilson controlled the ball beautifully with his instep, cut past a defender and crossed. The ball flew above the heads of the Lazio back four. As it bounced, Nat edged past Lazio right-back Franco Dessoti and toe-poked the ball past Paulo Calari.

GOAL!

Sixteen minutes on and I've scored!

Nat ran straight for the Rangers fans, waving his arms wildly. The fans went crazy, and when his teammates reached him, they pummelled him with joy. Ian Fox was screaming so loudly that Nat could pick his voice out among the thousands of others. But he wasn't celebrating – he was yelling at his players to get back into their own half for the Lazio kick off.

"OK, lads, that's enough!" commanded the Wildman. "We're back in the game. Let's get another goal!"

The next ten minutes were nervy ones. Lazio were determined to grab a third goal and kill off the game, and if it hadn't been for a quite superb save from Graham Dalston, they'd have had their way. His incredibly athletic dive, low and to his left, allowed him to make a fingertip save from a vicious Tassi bullet from just outside the Hatton Rangers penalty area.

From the resulting corner, Fellini went close with a header, but the Wildman hooked it off the line. Lazio now sensed victory was theirs for the taking and started firing in shots from all sorts of angles. Ian Fox was leaping about bellowing at his players to maintain possession and make some chances of their own.

By the eightieth minute, Rangers were starting to look slightly desperate and Adilson was reduced to taking a shot from sixty yards which went ridiculously wide. Nat was determined to create some havoc in the Lazio penalty area but the service to him and Robbie Clarke was almost non-existent, because the rest of the team were so busy defending. Nat made a decision – if he wasn't going to be passed the ball, he'd have to go and grab it for himself.

So when Lazio captain Ade Ragani stood over the ball on the halfway line, Nat sprinted over to him. Ragani saw him coming, but instead of passing, he shielded the ball with his body and leaned into Nat's challenge. Nat bounced off the defender, but recovered quickly and managed to get a touch on the ball. It rolled a couple of yards away from Ragani and Nat pounced. As Ragani tried to drag the ball back, Nat rounded him and pushed the ball further away. Ragani tugged at his shirt, but thankfully the referee played the advantage instead of blowing for a free kick.

Nat hared forward. He was accompanied by Clarke, Adilson, Jobson and Carigio who were all racing in his wake towards the Lazio penalty area. It was five against three Lazio defenders – Ade Ragani was off the pace.

"Yes, Nat!" screamed Jobson, who was now in the penalty area. Nat saw that Jobson was in the best position and released the ball. Jobson took it in his stride, but as he pulled back his leg to shoot, a massive lunging challenge from the Lazio keeper Calari sent him crashing to the ground. The ball rolled to Lazio's right-back, Franco Dessoti – who hacked it out of play.

The referee hadn't been brilliantly sighted, and for a couple of agonising seconds, Nat thought he'd just wave play on. But one of his assistants was waving his flag wildly. The referee nodded emphatically and pointed to the penalty spot. A split second later, he pulled out his red card and brandished it at Calari. The Lazio keeper went crazy, leaping up and jutting his head right into the referee's face. His teammates surrounded the referee, protesting that Calari's challenge was without malice and that he'd reached the ball.

But the referee was unmoved. He took several steps

back and shooed them away. Dean Jobson stood up. Calari ran after the official and carried on his protest. The Wildman ran over and put an arm round Calari's shoulder, but the Lazio keeper pushed him away and carried on shouting. The Wildman backed off.

The referee stood his ground, his finger still pointing to the touchline for Calari to follow. A furious and devastated Calari looked up to the heavens, and with a massive shake of his head, began the trudge towards the Lazio bench.

As Calari came off, one of the assistant referees held up an electronic board to indicate that Luigi Fellini would be coming off to enable Lazio to bring on their substitute keeper Oscar Piesca – a promising young ex-Juventus player who'd already represented Italy at under-twenty-one level.

Should I take the penalty? Nat wondered.

Dean Jobson ran to retrieve the ball and placed it on the penalty spot.

I guess not!

However, as soon as Jobson laid it down, Paulo Carigio raced up to him.

"Let Nat or Adilson take it!" he shouted.

Dean Jobson glared at him with disbelief. "I was fouled – I'm taking the penalty! And, in case you've forgotten, Adilson *missed* the last one!"

"This isn't playground football!" shouted Carigio. "There's too much at stake!"

"Back off, Paulo!" shouted Jobson with disgust.

Adilson, who'd been over by the bench, ran up to them.

"The boss wants me to take it," he declared.

Jobson stood there for a few seconds, looking as if he'd just been condemned to death. He then shoved Paulo Carigio in the chest and stormed off. But Carigio ran after him and shoved him back.

"Pack it in!" shouted the Wildman, coming between them. The combatants glared at each other for a few seconds and then strode away, seething, in opposite directions.

"OK, Adilson!" called the Wildman. "Take it and bury it!"

Adilson picked the ball up, rolled it over in his hands and placed it down again. He caught Nat's eyes and Nat clenched both fists at him in encouragement. Adilson nodded and tried to block his miss against Celtic out of his mind.

The referee was busy moving all of the Lazio players out of the area.

In the Lazio goal, Piesca waved his arms above his head and then stretched them out on either side of him. His big frame seemed to make the goal shrink. Adilson took a deep breath and walked back several paces.

Nat almost couldn't bear to watch. If Adilson missed, they'd be back in England tomorrow afternoon. But he kept his eyes open as Adilson took his run up.

The Brazilian struck the ball high and hard. For a second it looked like he'd skied it, but it dipped and crashed into the top right-hand corner of the Lazio net.

Adilson was mobbed by the Rangers players, with the notable exception of Dean Jobson, who was still steaming about the manager's decision to let Adilson take 'his' penalty. With Lazio now down to ten men, Hatton Rangers cashed in on their numerical advantage and kept everyone behind the ball. The Italians, roared on by their supporters and bench, tried desperately to break through the Rangers defensive wall but they had no luck. The referee ended the game on ninety minutes plus two added on.

It was over!

Two-two.

Hatton Rangers had just played themselves into their first ever final.

CHAPTER 25
The Shock

All eleven players and the subs ran over to their fans and applauded them wildly, and the fans reciprocated. Adilson was leaping in the air. He grabbed Nat, making it impossible for Nat not to join his crazy victory dance. The Wildman went to every player, slapping them on the back and uttering triumphant words of praise.

"We'll see you for the final!" called out the Wildman to the ecstatic supporters.

Stan Evans ran over and hugged Nat. "You were the difference, son!" he shouted in Nat's ear.

Back in the changing room, the players carried on their wild celebrations. There was singing and cheering and someone managed to get their hands on a bottle of champagne, which the Wildman opened and spayed round the changing room to whoops of delight.

"We've done it!" yelled Andy Young. "We're in the FINAL!"

Everyone cheered.

"Talorca beat Hamburg!" shouted Stan Evans, who had just been notified of this score by an El Mar official. "We're playing them on Saturday night!"

Nat gulped as he thought of Alberto Tieras and his gigantic frame. Playing against Tieras was going to be a massive challenge, whoever made it into the Rangers first eleven. Swinton's missing notebooks drifted into his brain for a few moments, but the euphoria of the win brought him back to the celebrations.

When Stan Evans finally got everyone quiet, Ian Fox walked into the centre of the room and indicated for everyone to sit down. It took a couple of minutes for the players to calm down, but then they were all sitting, waiting for the boss to speak. Nat had expected Fox to at least be cracking a smile or two, but he looked very serious.

"First of all, well done, lads," said the Rangers manager. "That was a very strong second half performance, and this time you followed my instructions to the letter. To get back from two-nil down is a big achievement."

The players clapped and cheered. Fox raised his hand and they stopped.

"However, my enjoyment on this historic occasion for Hatton Rangers Football Club was marred by what I saw after the penalty was granted."

There was instantly silence in the room.

"I've been in the game a long time," continued Fox, "and I've known certain players who don't see eye-to-eye with each other, but unfortunately what we saw tonight is just one in a number of incidents that have occurred between Misters Jobson and Carigio."

He eyed Dean and then Paulo. They both looked down at the floor.

"I've stuck by you as a pairing in spite of the many squabbles you've had, but tonight was the lowest point. We're out here in Spain, representing not only our club, but English football, and you two behaved in a disgraceful way. We were given a penalty and then two things happened. First, Dean ran to get the ball because he thought that as he was fouled it was *his* penalty. Dean, I needn't remind you that you are not our first, our second or even our third penalty-taker. And then Paulo, instead of waiting for me or the Wildman to make matters straight, you got in Dean's face. What the hell did you think you were doing? Did you think that would help team harmony?"

Lots of other players, including Nat were now looking at the ground too. The atmosphere was tense and very uncomfortable.

"I will *not* have a repeat of what happened here tonight. I will *not* have two of my players arguing like school kids at a critical point in a match. I know it wasn't a Premier League or an FA Cup game, but I told you how seriously I wanted this tournament to be taken. Your antics were a kick in the face, not just to Stan and me, but to the entire team. For that reason, I'm sending you both home."

It was as if a bomb had just splintered the room apart. There were gasps of shock from everyone, including Stan Evans, who clearly hadn't known that the boss was about to drop this stick of dynamite. Nat looked up and gaped at Ian Fox.

I know what they did was out of order, but sending them home? They're both internationals. They're both vastly experienced. They're both top players. Surely you don't need to make their punishment this radical?

"Hang on a second, boss," began the Wildman, but Fox held up a finger to indicate that, on this occasion, even the Wildman should remain silent.

"There's an eleven o'clock flight from Talorca to Heathrow," said Fox. "I want you both on it. I'll talk to you when the rest of us are back in England. Take your stuff and go. A car is waiting for you next to the team bus – *if* you can be trusted to travel in the same vehicle."

Jobson and Carigio both looked totally shaken. They stood with all eyes on them, got their things together and shuffled out of the changing room. Carigio turned back to the rest of the team and managed a small wave goodbye. Jobson didn't look back. A few seconds later they were gone.

The room stayed deathly silent until Fox spoke again.

"Believe me, lads, I didn't want to do that, but I have no choice. I can't have those two squabbling for the whole world to see – it's not just bad for PR, it's bad for everyone's morale. It means our squad is now slimmed down to sixteen and we've lost two first-rate internationals, but it's a point of principle, and maybe we can come out on the other side of this with Jobson and Carigio having finally put their feud to rest. If they can't do that, then I'm afraid I'm going to transfer-list them and buy replacements."

The silence deepened.

"With them gone," went on Fox, "there will be some good opportunities for the rest of you. I know I said before the tournament that I wanted to establish a solid first eleven but sometimes events take over. We now need to be more flexible. Play well, show commitment and you never know what might happen."

The manager's eyes rested on Nat for a split second.

Is he talking about me? I definitely delivered tonight and with those two gone, who knows?

By the time the players walked out of the changing room, the celebratory air had been tempered by the removal of Jobson and Carigio from the squad. It wouldn't be long before the story hit the wires and the British press would be all over it.

Evans ushered the players into the warm Spanish night. A few stopped to sign autographs for Hatton Rangers fans, and for them they kept up their expressions of good cheer and bonhomie. When the fans found out about Jobson and Carigio, they wouldn't be too pleased with Ian Fox, irrespective of the penalty fiasco.

Nat was about to climb onto the bus behind Kelvin, when something suddenly caught his eye.

It was the man – the one he'd seen in the stands in the first training session.

CHAPTER 26
A Mystery Chase and
a Night-time Excursion

A tremor shot through Nat. The man was just about to walk down into an underpass at the end of the street about a hundred metres away.

Nat thought fast. Should he tell Fox and Evans? He looked over his shoulder. They hadn't come out of the stadium yet. Should he grab a policeman? There were a couple by the entrance to the turnstiles, chatting good-naturedly to Lazio fans. He could approach them, but his Spanish was nowhere near good enough to explain the situation, and besides, even if he could, what reason would he give them for chasing the man? That he'd seen him once before at training and didn't like the look of him?

No, there was only one thing for it. Nat dropped his bag and ran.

Thoughts of Tanner and Chris Webb flooded into his mind as he pounded the pavement. He remembered Tanner picking up a gun. He remembered the bottle he'd grabbed from the cleaning trolley and sprayed in Tanner's face. That spray had saved his life. If this man was connected in any way to Tanner or the people behind the match-fixing scheme, he had to be careful. He couldn't have this thing hanging over him, but if things looked too dangerous he would have to stop and call for help.

A few stalls selling snacks were dotted along the pavement. Nat sprinted past these and spied a small gaggle of Hatton Rangers fans up ahead on the kerb, trying to wave down a taxi. One of them spotted him and stepped in his way.

"Sorry, I can't stop," said Nat, skirting round him. The lad shouted after him, but he couldn't hear what he said.

The man Nat was chasing had now disappeared into the subway.

I might have a chance of reaching him if I'm fast!

Onwards Nat's feet took him. He nearly sent an elderly man flying, but managed to skid out of his way at the last second. He was almost at the entrance to the subway, and as he reached it, he grabbed the railings, pulled himself round and leapt down the stairs, four at a time.

At the bottom was a long tunnel, lit by the dim glow of some faint yellow lights, similar to the ones used on the London Underground. The man was about sixty metres away, but as Nat charged forward he took a sharp left and vanished from view.

Increasing his pace, Nat rushed past a woman with a pram who was talking on her mobile and overtook two teenage girls who were laughing loudly. Finally he reached the spot where the man had turned left.

He stopped abruptly. In front of him were three new

tunnels, each one turning sharply and so preventing Nat from seeing down them. He stamped his foot in frustration and made an instant decision – he plunged into the left one, following its curve round. But to his disappointment, when it straightened out, the only person ahead of him was an elderly woman pulling a battered shopping trolley behind her.

Nat retraced his steps and sprinted into the middle tunnel, but this was empty. Back again he ran and entered the tunnel on the right. This curved, led under the road and then ascended back up to street level. Nat rushed up the steps and frantically looked in all directions.

There was no sign of the man.

Damn!

Nat winced with frustration and started walking back to the team bus and his fellow players. They'd be wondering why on earth he'd raced off in such a hurry, but he was in no mood to tell them anything about the chase.

When he reached the bus, Stan Evans was standing at the door checking his watch.

"There you are!" he exclaimed. "Kelvin said that one minute you were about to get on the bus and the next you raced off somewhere."

"I just thought I saw someone I knew," panted Nat, stepping past Evans and climbing onto the bus.

"Who was it?" enquired Evans, following him on.

"Just someone I met at my host's house. It doesn't matter."

Nat was sorely tempted to share his suspicions with

Stan, but once again he remained silent. Even though he was scared, fear of making himself look like a paranoid madman held him back.

"Whatever you say," replied Evans, whose mind was now on ensuring that all of his players and staff were on board.

On the journey back to the team hotel, Nat tried to concentrate on the conversation he was having with Kelvin and Emi, but his mind kept darting back to the mystery man.

Who is he, and is he connected to Tanner and the match-fixing scam?

The team bus dropped him off on the coastal road and he walked the rest of the way back to Inés's place. It was quiet when he got in. The light in Inés's room was off but a line of light spilled out from under José's door.

Nat went on to his room and picked up his book. A few pages in and he'd been drawn back into the twists and turns of the lightning-paced plot, and after forty minutes he felt his eyelids drooping. The book slipped out of his hand onto the floor and he was just about to flick off his bedside light when he heard soft footsteps outside his window.

Must be a fox or some other kind of night creature.

But the footsteps were too loud for an animal. Out of curiosity, Nat checked his watch. It was 12.28 a.m. Who was wandering around at this hour? Although his body screamed out for him to ignore it and go to sleep, he forced himself out of bed, crossed the room and pulled back the blinds. There was José, walking away from the house with a small rucksack on his back.

Nat knew he should just climb back into bed but he was intrigued. José looked as if he was setting off on a hike . . . well after midnight. Without really knowing what he was doing, Nat tiptoed out of his room and hurried down the corridor, letting himself out of the front door as quietly as he could. He left the door on the latch so that he'd be able to get in again.

He crept out into the warm night, walking quickly through the courtyard to the back of the house. José was climbing the bare hill about thirty metres ahead of him. When José looked round, Nat threw himself onto the ground, hoping he hadn't been seen. But when he raised his head, José was gone. Nat tutted in frustration and started running silently up the hill. When he came to its brow, at first he couldn't see José, but then he spied him walking along a narrow path onto a patch of scrubland. After fifty metres, José knelt down on the ground. Nat held back, crouching down by the base of an olive tree. But a few moments later, José had completely disappeared from view – it was as if the scrubland had swallowed him.

Making as little noise as possible, Nat quickly stole over to where José had been crouching. There on the ground was an open wooden trapdoor. It must have been buried beneath some earth. That's what José had been doing when he knelt down – he'd been moving the dry mud to reveal the door. Nat peered down into the hole but couldn't see anything.

What on earth is he doing down there?

He then heard the scraping of feet. José was coming back. If José spotted him it would undoubtedly lead to a very unpleasant scene. José had been furious with his mother for talking to Nat about him. He'd surely go completely crazy if he discovered Nat had followed him out here. But as Nat's brain was computing his next move, an unsettling thought suddenly hit him. He'd left the front door on the latch – he had to get back to the villa first otherwise José would see this and also notice that Nat's bedroom door was open. He should have shut it!

But the scrubland was very open. The moon was bright enough to illuminate it and José would be appearing in a few seconds – he'd surely see Nat running ahead. That left only one option. Nat would have to sprint to the fence at the left side of the land, which was quite near, get over it, and somehow cut back to the villa, hoping there were no major obstacles in the way and he could beat José there.

As José reached up to the door to pull himself back out, Nat sprinted towards the fence. He looked back for a second and saw José's head emerging. Luckily he was facing the other way or he'd have seen Nat. Nat spotted several red discs spread out along the fence. It was electrified. He didn't fancy getting a high-voltage shock, but it was too late to change his mind – José would definitely see him if he turned round now. So Nat sped up, clenched his teeth, made his best Olympic-hurdles-style jump and cleared the fence by a few millimetres. He landed in a clump of thorny bushes, and to his horror saw that the whole field was covered in these shrubs. But that was tough luck – he *had* to get back before José. He sprinted in the general direction of the villa, the thorns snagging him. His hands took quite a few hits but he powered on, finally reaching another fence, also electrified. But this time he wasn't jumping from flat ground, he was jumping from a field full of thorn bushes.

As a result, his leap wasn't as powerful and his left trainer got caught on the wire. He crashed to the ground and felt his leg yanking him back. The bottom of his pyjama trousers was pulled up and his shin came into contact with the metal. A large jolt of electricity fizzed through him. In panic he grabbed his leg and pulled. Luckily, his twisting movement released his trainer and his leg fell down to join the rest of his body.

The effect of the shock was still fizzing, but he managed to pull himself up and, to his relief, saw the field he was now in had no bushes – it was just scrubland. And there, up ahead, was the villa. He raced forwards, looking to his right, where José should be appearing in a few seconds. And sure enough, it wasn't long before José's figure came into view at the top of the hill. Nat hurried on, hoping José couldn't see him as he crashed down towards the villa. He ran round to the front door, slipped inside, took the door off the latch and closed it quickly.

"Nat?" Inés's voice made him jolt with shock.

She flicked a switch and light flooded into the hallway. Nat instinctively placed his hands behind his back to hide the scratches he'd picked up from the vicious thorn bushes.

"I was just going to the bathroom," explained Nat.

"You've gone past it," Inés pointed out.

"You know how it is when you wake up in a place you don't know that well?" he bluffed.

She arched an eyebrow suspiciously, and watched as Nat hurried towards the bathroom. She turned off the corridor light as he entered the bathroom. Once inside, he switched on the bathroom light. Nat listened for the sound of José returning.

But José didn't come back.

Did he see me outside? thought Nat frantically. *Or did he see the corridor light and now the bathroom light go on? Maybe he's waiting for all of the lights to go out?*

Nat took a deep breath, flushed the toilet and walked out of the bathroom, turning off the light as he went. He returned to his room and lay in the darkness, waiting for José's footsteps. But they didn't arrive, or at least he didn't hear them, before he fell asleep.

CHAPTER 27
A Criminal Checks In

Ray Swinton was just finishing off a late-night coffee in a small corner bar in Talorca town centre when his phone rang.

"Mr Swinton," said the Eastern European voice.

"Surprise, surprise," answered Swinton, his voice dripping with sarcasm. "Going to do the right thing and give me back what's rightfully mine?"

"I'm just checking to see if we're still on for tomorrow night and that you haven't contacted any of the law agencies of this country."

"No," snapped back Swinton. "I did consider phoning the air force but their helicopters are a bit too big to land in Talorca's central bus station."

"If you think you are being funny, you are not," said the voice coldly. "We have a business agreement and I need to be sure you will be there, with the money, at the right time."

Swinton sighed wearily and wiped his brow. "I'll be there," he replied testily, "and there'll be no policemen lurking round any corners. It will just be me and the money, and you and the notebooks, OK?"

"That is what we agreed," responded the voice.

"I'll see you there," said Swinton.

The line went dead.

CHAPTER 28
The Threat

The following morning Nat got up early. The villa was quiet. Both Inés's and José's doors were closed. Nat stole down the corridor and exited the villa. He retraced his steps of the night before, up the hill and across the scrubland. There were no landmarks to indicate exactly where the trapdoor was, so he approximated the position and started clawing at the earth with his fingers. His first bout of digging revealed nothing, so he moved and tried again. This was unsuccessful too, but on his third try, his fingernails came into contact with wood. He quickly scraped the rest of the earth away to reveal the wooden trapdoor.

He pulled at the steel circle on its surface. The door flipped up and onto the ground, revealing the hole below. Nat took a quick look round to make sure he wasn't being watched, and lowered himself inside.

At the bottom was a tiny passage. There was just enough room for him to crouch down and crawl through it. At its end was a small opening, on the floor of which was the rucksack Nat had seen José carrying the night before. He pulled open the zip and looked inside. The only thing in the rucksack was an A4-sized plastic pocket containing several sheaves of yellowing paper. He pulled these out and checked them over. The first lot were covered in Spanish writing, some done on a computer, some written by hand. These were followed by some spreadsheets, also in Spanish.

But at the bottom of the pile were several large fold-out technical drawings. At the top right-hand corner of each illustration was the words *La Plaza* – the home stadium of Talorca FC. Some were drawings of the entire structure, others were cross-sectional drawings of parts of it. One image particularly caught Nat's eye. It was a drawing of the stadium's executive car park – Nat could see this by the superimposed images of top-of-the-range vehicles in parking bays. There were several comments in Spanish scribbled in blue ink at the top of the page, next to Sunday's date.

Nat's mind worked furiously as he tried to piece together the jigsaw. It gradually started to make sense. Sunday was the day after the tournament final. On Sunday, a huge lunch was being hosted at the stadium by Victor Mabena for the two teams who'd reached the final – Hatton Rangers and Talorca FC. While Mabena and his fellow board members were busy at the lunch, José (and, presumably, some accomplices) would be in the executive car park, stealing their top-of-the-range cars. That had to be it! And that was why José was so interested in the car manuals – he was figuring out how best to start them without the keys.

It was the perfect crime. On match days there would be loads of security around La Plaza, but this was a Sunday. Security would presumably be miniscule by comparison. José had already made it clear that he hated Mabena and the money men of the club, and this must be his way of getting back at them. Selling such cars on would also be a very healthy source of cash for José, who had no other obvious income. The money José had been holding must have come from his last job. He was a high-end car thief!

What should I do? Confront José and say I know all about it? No, that way he'll know I've been spying on him and he'll go completely crazy. Tell Inés? Show her this place?

It was impossible. José's life had already been messed up by the accident. Could Nat ruin it even further by getting him in serious trouble?

Nat sighed, carefully replaced the papers inside the rucksack and put it down on the floor. He reached up and pulled himself out of the hole. He flipped the trapdoor shut and set about re-covering it in earth. He hurried back to the villa with several burning yet unanswerable questions rattling around in his head.

On his return, he found Inés and José at the kitchen table, poring over an article in the newspaper. They both looked up guiltily when he came in.

"What is it?" asked Nat, worried for a second that *they'd* been spying on *him*.

"It's just something in today's paper," said Inés, folding it hurriedly.

"You should tell him," said José. "He's got a right to know."

"To know what?" asked Nat.

Had the moment finally arrived when the truth about his real age was paraded before the world? Had Ray Swinton broken his word and unleashed mayhem that would scupper all of Nat's football dreams?

"Please tell me," he said anxiously.

"OK," sighed Inés, "but I don't feel very comfortable about it."

"Just read it," urged José.

Reluctantly, Inés opened the paper up once again, studied the text for a few seconds and then began translating into English.

Talorca stalwart and captain Alberto Tieras has had a busy week. As well as leading his team to the final of a tournament involving some of Europe's best teams, he also had a lot of fun winding up two players from the English team, Hatton Rangers, whom he will now be facing in Saturday night's final. Appearing on a local radio show, the two young players were stunned when Tieras showed up in the studio and they stormed out when his jibes got the better of them.

Inés looked up to gauge Nat's reaction. He nodded at her to go on.

With Hatton Rangers now facing Talorca in the final,

Tieras was in a particularly upbeat mood at the team's training ground yesterday. He had some words of warning, particularly for one of the players he met in the studio.

"The English team, whose name I can't remember because they are so low-profile, have a young player called Nat Dixon, and this boy is very arrogant. He swaggers around with the air of one who has seen many campaigns, when in fact he has only played a few times for his club. While the two strikers in front of him at the club are the first choice pairing, this Dixon kid has come on as a substitute in both games so far and made something of an 'impact'. Well, the child can forget about making any such impact this Saturday night because he will be playing against the big boys! If he does come on and try anything fancy, he will very soon be looking at a stretcher – the one that is carrying him off the pitch!"

Tieras's words are always strong, but this outburst was one of his most ferocious. Little is known about Nat Dixon, other than that he was scouted playing street soccer in the US and was bought by Rangers's manager Ian Fox in this year's January transfer window. Due to some hold-up in his paperwork he was only able to play for his team in the last few games of the season, when he also made a big impact, scoring the goal that saved his club from relegation on the very last day of the season.

Nat looked at Inés and José in amazement. "That's pretty strong," he said in shock.

"It's a disgrace!" exploded Inés. "How dare he say such things? These comments should be reported to the police – talking about a stretcher! That's threatening you with violence! Footballers need to observe the same laws as the rest of us. If he went onto the street and said something like that, he'd be immediately arrested."

"He's all mouth," muttered José. "Ignore him."

"That's easier said than done," tutted Inés.

"Anyway," said José, "the tournament's over on Saturday and hopefully Nat won't have to hear any more of this rubbish from Tieras or Victor Mabena or anyone connected to the club."

There it was again – José's hatred of Mabena. Well now Nat knew that José would be punishing Mabena on Sunday when he stole his car, and probably those of some of his cronies too.

As Nat helped Inés with the washing-up, he kept thinking about how a supposedly straightforward trip to Spain had become so complicated. First there was his stalker, then there was Alberto Tieras, and Ray Swinton's missing notebooks. And now there was José's car-stealing plan. It felt like the dream jaunt had become a bit of a nightmare.

CHAPTER 29
Protect and Survive

"Nat?"

"Hey Dad." It was a couple of hours after Nat's early morning hunt and the sun's heat was already hitting the villa.

"I have some excellent news."

"What?"

"We've finished the first part of the job early. They don't need me this weekend, so guess what? I'm flying out to Spain tomorrow morning."

"Are you serious?" asked Nat, suddenly feeling a wave of relief and joy.

"I get to Talorca airport at half past eleven in the morning."

"That's great," said Nat. "Talorca are training at La Plaza from nine to ten thirty. Then we've got it from eleven thirty until one and after that we'll be at the team hotel. Fox has said that families can visit us in the hotel between two and four."

"Perfect. I'll come to the hotel."

"Where are you staying?"

"A small hotel on the outskirts of Talorca. Stan Evans has already sorted me out with a ticket for the match."

"Excellent! I'm really pleased you're coming, but I don't know if I'll get on the pitch."

"Nonsense," said Dave. "You've done wonders out there. I'm sure you'll get a decent run out. Fox knows what you can do."

Nat paused. There was so much he wanted to tell his dad.

"What's up?" asked Dave.

"Er . . . nothing."

"Doesn't sound like nothing."

"It's just . . . Alberto Tieras – you know, the Talorca captain."

"What's he been up to?"

"There was a thing on Wednesday when he kind of hijacked a radio interview Emi and I were doing, and then in the paper today there was a quote from him about putting me on a stretcher."

"A *stretcher*?" exploded Dave. "How dare he?"

"Apparently that's what he's always like – he loves intimidating opponents."

"But he mentioned you by name?"

"Yeah."

"If he lays one finger on you, I'll be on him!"

"Maybe we should leave things to the ref?"

"OK, but I'll be watching him like a hawk."

"I know you will. Anyway, I'll see you at the hotel at two, yeah?"

"Absolutely. You just need to win to make my trip worthwhile."

Nat laughed, pleased he'd at least mentioned one of his current worries to his dad.

* * *

"Well done, everyone!" Stan Evans called out, as the players came to the end of a series of runs and sprints. Nat took a swig from a water bottle and sat down on the grass with the others. He'd been on top form again during training, buoyed by the news of his dad coming over the next day. He was looking forward to training at La Plaza too.

This was Rangers's last training session on the El Mar pitch. Tomorrow – the day of the final – they'd have their session at La Plaza.

"OK, gentlemen," said Ian Fox. "With Jobson and Carigio gone, I've decided to switch things around for the final – give Talorca a bit of a surprise."

Nat raised an eyebrow at Emi.

"We're going to play four-three-two-one. I know we've never played that system before, but Stan and I think it's the right team shape for this particular match. So I'm going to announce the team now and we're going to work on the basis of this new formation, OK?"

The players nodded, some of them a bit uncertainly. Nat felt a spark of hope. This could be good news for him. Had the manager opted to play Jensen up front, with him and Robbie Clarke as the two behind him? That would be superb!

"So, Dalston stays in goal and our back four remain the same. In midfield, we're going to play Adilson on the left, Luke Summers on the right and Clifton in the middle. Up front will be Clarke and Sinclair as the two strikers playing behind Jensen."

Nat felt the colour drain from his cheeks. Fox had just placed Nicky Sinclair ahead of him in the pecking order! What the hell was he playing at? Surely Nat was miles ahead of Sinclair? Nicky was a decent player but he'd hardly stamped his personality on the training sessions and his form had been very shaky. Why was Fox doing this – did he think Nat was getting above his station because he'd put in a couple of decent substitute appearances? Fox didn't need to play psychological games with him – if that was it, it was pathetic!

For the rest of the session, Nat was in a foul mood, although he tried desperately not to show it. In the five-a-sides he played like a man possessed, running harder than any of the other forwards and shooting with power and accuracy.

I'll show Fox he's making the biggest mistake of his life!

Nicky Sinclair had a few nice touches, but both of his shots went wide. In the last few seconds of the final game, Nat scored with a blistering strike that flashed past a fully-stretched Jack Bell. But when it was all over, Nat's buoyancy over his good show in the games was replaced by the cold emotion of disappointment.

Fox wasn't going to change his mind. He'd gone with Nicky Sinclair and there was nothing Nat could do about it.

As the players trooped back towards the tunnel, Kelvin caught up with Nat.

"I haven't got a clue what Fox is doing," whispered Kelvin, making sure his words were well out of the manager's earshot. "I can't believe he's put Nicky in there instead of you. We need you, man!"

Before Nat could reply, he felt a tap on his shoulder. He span round and came face-to-face with Ian Fox.

"See you in a minute," Nat mouthed at Kelvin, who nodded guiltily and disappeared into the tunnel.

"Come and sit down for a minute," said Fox. They walked over to the technical area and sat down on the home team's bench.

"You're angry about Sinclair getting the nod instead of you?" asked Fox.

"Is it that obvious?"

"Just short of having a sign painted on your face."

Nat grimaced. "I've played better than Nicky this week. He's only had a few minutes on the pitch as a sub without doing that much. I've come on and made a difference."

"My decision isn't based on strictly football reasons."

Nat frowned.

"There are several things I factored in when I selected tomorrow night's side. I know I don't need to explain myself to you, but I'm always aware of your 'situation', so I want to put you in the picture."

Nat sighed deeply, keen to hear what the boss had to say.

"You've really picked up over the week," went on Fox. "Your attitude and performances have risen to a good level."

Finally, a bit of praise from the manager!

"But tomorrow night La Plaza will be a cauldron. It will be packed to the rafters and the crowd will really get behind their team. I mean, they'll be making some serious noise."

"I can handle it, boss," said Nat, aware that his voice sounded slightly desperate.

"That's for me to decide," replied Fox firmly. "I read what Alberto Tieras said about you in the papers. And while I'm not one to allow big-mouthed opposition players to dictate who I choose to play, Tieras is a fearsome battler, and for some reason he's got it into his thick head that you're some kind of threat to him, and that he'll cause you damage. If he goes for you, you could easily sustain a career-threatening injury."

"But surely if I want to develop as a player, I need to face people like Tieras?"

"On one level you're right, Nat, but I don't feel I can risk putting you on at the start. Tieras will head straight for you and anything could happen. I don't want to be responsible for that."

"But aren't risks a central part of the game?" asked Nat.

"There are risks and there are risks," answered Fox.

"And don't forget, I've only said I don't want you *starting* the match, I haven't said I won't use you at all. I just want Tieras to have exerted himself a bit before I think about bringing you on. You'll have better luck against him if he's already made twenty challenges."

"But . . . but . . . does this mean that every time a defender says he's going to mark me out of a game I'll go straight to the back of the queue?"

"Of course it doesn't, but we must remember. . ." He lowered his voice. "You're thirteen, Nat, and I'm not taking any chances. You'll be on the bench but there's a strong possibility you'll get on. I can't say fairer than that."

Nat tried to rationalise Fox's position, but it was hard to see beyond the fact that he'd done much better than Sinclair and his only reward was for Sinclair to jump ahead of him in the queue.

Talk about unfair!

"I need to make sure that you're not exposed to things before you're ready," said Fox, standing up. "Now go in there, get changed with the rest of the lads and be in the best mental and physical shape for tomorrow night. We have a final to play for the first time in this club's history and we're going to give it our all."

As the Hatton Rangers players walked out of the building to the team bus, another group of Spanish teenagers were waiting for them. They ran over and got as many Rangers players to sign pieces of paper and old football programmes as they could. An elderly man walked over to Nat and spoke to him in broken English.

"I am Talorca FC supporter."

"Hi," nodded Nat.

"But I do not like what Tieras says about you."

"Thanks."

"He is big mouth. You are young player. You go out and play good football, yes?"

"Yes!" smiled Nat. He shook the man's hand. At least it wasn't just him and the Rangers party who thought Tieras was a nightmare.

Stan Evans slotted down into the seat next to Nat on the team bus.

"The boss said he had a word with you about Tieras."

Nat nodded. "He told me I didn't make the starting line-up because he was protecting me – something along those lines."

"Absolutely," said Evans. "I just wanted to let you know that we've made a formal complaint to Talorca FC about Tieras's quote in the Spanish press today and his behaviour at the radio station. We're appalled by it and we've let them know our position before the match."

"Have Talorca got back to you?"

"Not yet, but we've laid down a marker. We've also made it very clear that we'll be watching every move Tieras makes. If – or when – you get onto the pitch and he in any way tries to deliberately injure you, we'll be on to him in a second. We're also going to speak to the referee before kick off. We want him to know the situation – be on his guard for Tieras."

"Thanks," said Nat.

Evans grinned. "You don't have to thank us – just do your best if you get onto the pitch, like you did in the other two games. You don't have to worry about Tieras."

Nat let out a breath of relief. It was far better that it was all out in the open and that Fox and Evans were going to be looking out for him.

All he needed now was to get a game.

CHAPTER 30
Handover

A man named Gregor, with an Eastern European accent, wearing a long brown raincoat, large sunglasses and a coat of stubble on his face, arrived at Talorca's central bus station at 7.15 p.m. He'd arrived early because he wanted to spot the journalist Ray Swinton, before Swinton saw him. He'd found several recent pictures of Swinton on the internet and had studied them carefully.

He headed round a large group of women wearing multi-coloured wigs, a tall blind man with dark glasses, a panama hat and a white stick, and a huddle of teenage boys in hoodies. A guard went hurrying by, holding a two-way radio and looking harassed. Gregor calmly walked past the stops for the number forty-five and number seventy-seven buses, and then studied a large poster on the back of the stop for the number twelve. It showed a luxurious beach with golden sand and a turquoise sky. If all went well here, before the night was out, he would have an extra £10,000 to play with. That would pay for a couple of nice holidays.

He thought about his two phone calls with Swinton.

The *Sunday Crest* journalist had come over as tough and combative, but those notebooks with their hundreds of scribbles and jottings and roughly-sketched diagrams must be vitally important to the man if he'd agreed to hand over such a substantial sum of cash. They looked like they represented years of work. Gregor was pretty sure that Swinton would stick to his word and be there alone, but that didn't stop him from casting his eyes around – looking out for any plain clothes police officers. In Gregor's experience, they were generally easy to spot because of the somewhat mismatched outfits they wore to 'fit in'.

At 7.30 on the dot, Gregor spotted Swinton at the number twenty-eight bus stop. The *Sunday Crest* journalist was standing with his back against the wall, holding a thick white envelope tightly in his right hand, just as Gregor had instructed. His facial expression gave away nothing as he glanced at his watch. He was alone and there was no one close to him who looked anything like a police officer.

Gregor stood by a bench, waiting while a bus pulled into the stop. Some people got on, others got off. Gregor stayed exactly where he was, keeping a beady eye on the journalist. The bus moved on and when it had disappeared round the corner, Gregor started walking towards Swinton. When he reached him, he stood beside him and in a low voice said, "Can I have the envelope please?"

Swinton immediately handed it over. Gregor checked

both ways down to see if any police officers had suddenly appeared, but all was quiet. He quickly slit open the envelope and looked inside. There were three large bundles of euro notes. He flicked through them rapidly to make sure they were real and that they added up to the agreed sum. He'd once been stung by a handover where the only genuine notes were the ones on top of the bundles and the ones below had been fakes.

Satisfied that this cash was real, and after checking around them again, Gregor placed the envelope in one of the inside pockets of his coat. He was now in possession of £10,000 in euros. He reached inside a larger pocket and produced a plastic bag with the notebooks. It was now Swinton's turn to do some checking. He looked at each of the notebooks, checking carefully to see that no pages had been ripped out or replaced. When he'd seen that all was in order, he turned to face Gregor.

"Did you or any of your 'colleagues' copy any pages?" he asked.

"None," replied Gregor. "They are intact and they have not been tampered with. This is a one-off deal. There will be no second demand."

"There better not be!" growled Swinton.

"Our business is concluded," said Gregor curtly. "You now go the way you came and don't look back."

Swinton stared at him for a couple of seconds and then moved off. Gregor watched him for over a minute, by which time he'd disappeared from view. Gregor then began to stride back in the direction he'd come, a feeling of deep elation spreading through his veins as it did after every 'job'. He couldn't help but praise himself and his masterful planning, and he was particularly delighted with this end of the deal. Swinton had been a walkover. Gregor was already planning his next job in his head and, emboldened by this one, he now intended to hit a higher-profile victim, possibly a celebrity who would pay a far larger amount for the return of their personal documents.

Gregor saw a number seventy-seven bus pulling in to its stop and he quickly headed towards it. The women with the coloured wigs and the blind man also got on. They all proceeded to the standing room in the centre of the bus. It was hot and crowded. The bus passed a couple of stops but pulled in at the third. The blind man moved towards the doors. As he did so, he stumbled and fell forward, barging into Gregor's shoulder.

"*Lo siento*," said the blind man apologetically, straightening up.

Gregor scowled but said nothing. The man climbed off the bus, his stick tapping out its rhythm as he headed along the pavement.

It was only after the bus had pulled away from its seventh stop that Gregor checked his jacket pocket and discovered to his horror that the cash-stuffed envelope had gone.

CHAPTER 31
The Plan that Worked

As Gregor frantically searched his jacket pockets and his bus sped on, Ray Swinton sat sipping a coffee at the bus station's large cafe. He looked up when he heard the tapping of a white stick and spotted the blind man weaving his way through the crowds.

The man stopped when he was right next to Swinton.

"How did it go?" asked Swinton.

"Piece of cake," replied the man, pulling off his sunglasses and panama hat to reveal Nat.

After Swinton had told him about the blackmail demand and had outlined Nat's possible role in the 'handover', he had initially said no. Dressing up as a blind man and stealing the money back from an Eastern European crook wasn't really his scene – it was more for the characters who appeared in the thrillers he liked to read. But Swinton had pointed out the necessity of keeping this 'matter' small and, as Nat's name featured in the notebooks, it was in his interests to help get them back. Swinton had shown him how to stumble, barge and reach inside someone's jacket to pilfer items. He said he'd picked it up when he did his RAF training, but Nat wasn't sure he believed him. However, this hadn't stopped him finally agreeing to the plan and, unseen by anyone else, Nat had practised a lot. To his relief, he'd got it right when it mattered.

"But don't you think he'll come after us with his mates?" asked Nat nervously. Swinton left some money for his coffee and they headed out of the cafe and back in the direction of the hotels.

"Very unlikely," replied Swinton. "If we see him again and alert the police he'll be in a lot of bother. The police might even be looking for him already. You can bet that this wasn't the first scam he's tried to pull off. I'd love to see his face when he realises the money's gone!"

Swinton laughed heartily.

"Do you think he showed them to anyone else?" asked Nat.

"No," replied Swinton. "He's a chancer – he was probably just calling my bluff that he would have shown them at all. And anyway, I told you – my handwriting's pretty illegible. I've got my notebooks back, you got the cash back for me, all we need to do now is get Hatton Rangers to beat Talorca tomorrow night and the world will be perfect! I still can't believe the team made it to a final. If you'd told me a few years back that Rangers would be in this position, I'd have laughed you out of the room."

They walked for the next twenty minutes until they reached an intersection.

"My hotel's that way," said Swinton. "I'll see you at the game tomorrow. Are you going to tell me the line-up?"

"You must be joking," replied Nat. "The gaffer would kill me. He'll tell you in his own good time."

"Suit yourself," said Swinton. "I'll see you tomorrow. I'm going to do some post-match interviews with the lads after the final. Will you be getting a game?"

"Don't try and trick me!" said Nat with a wry smile.

"Well, if I don't see you before the game, viva Hatton Rangers!" laughed Swinton.

"Yeah, something like that," said Nat.

"You did brilliantly with that criminal," said Swinton. "I owe you one."

They shook hands and parted.

CHAPTER 32
An Unwelcome Knock

It was late Friday night. Carlos and Rudy were dog-tired but they couldn't stop – not yet.

"It will all be worth it," said Carlos, looking up from the table where he was working, a laptop open and several empty mugs scattered round.

"I know," replied Rudy.

Earlier, Rudy had seen the bald man carrying some office furniture into the unit he'd rented, along the corridor. The man hadn't seen him.

Half an hour later, they were on the verge of packing up when the buzzer to their unit went. They looked at each other. They then looked at the table. It was completely covered.

"What shall we do?" mouthed Rudy.

"We have to answer it," whispered Carlos. "It could be the bald man – he might just want to say hello."

"It's past midnight," said Rudy grimly. "A weird time for introductions, don't you think?"

"But our lights are on," pointed out Carlos. "It would be more suspicious not to answer it."

The buzzer went again.

"You get it," said Carlos.

A few seconds later, Rudy opened the door a fraction and looked out. He was staggered to see two police officers standing there, ID cards in hand.

"I'm Officer Pedro," said the man standing in front, "and this is Officer Carez."

"How can I help you?" asked Rudy, aware of the slight wobble in his voice which betrayed his anxiety.

"Could we come in for a moment?" asked Pedro.

Rudy heard Carlos frantically clearing the table behind him. Panic gripped his throat. What if the officers saw anything? What if they recognised Carlos as the prison escaper?

"Can I ask what this is about?" Rudy said.

"We'd prefer to come inside," said Carez.

Rudy knew that to say no was out of the question. "Sure," he said, "please come in."

He turned round, half-expecting Carlos to be throwing things out of the window, but to his immense relief, the table was cleared and Carlos was sitting on a chair, wearing a black beanie hat quite low over his face and flicking through the day's paper.

Rudy went to sit next to Carlos, and indicated for the policemen to join them, but the officers remained standing. Rudy was shaking and just hoped this wasn't visible to Pedro and Carez.

"We've received a report of unusual activity in this block," said Pedro.

Rudy felt as if the air had just been squeezed out of his body. Carlos cleared his throat.

"What sort of activity?" enquired Carlos, making his voice deeper than usual.

"Illegal activity," replied Pedro.

Rudy gulped. They were on to them. It was all over. Carlos would be going back to prison and Rudy would be joining him.

"It's connected to the other unit on this floor that's just been rented out," explained Carez.

Rudy almost cried out with delight.

"We wanted to know if you'd seen anything suspicious."

"Suspicious in what way?" asked Rudy.

"I'm afraid we can't divulge that," replied Carez.

"I haven't seen anything," said Carlos, turning to Rudy. "Have you?"

"Nothing," agreed Rudy, "I've only seen the other tenant once."

"Fine," nodded Carez. "We're just doing some routine enquiries. If you do see anything, can you give us a call?"

He handed his card to Carlos.

"Of course, officer," replied Carlos, standing up and taking the card. He strolled back to the door with them.

"Well, thank you," said Carez, "and sorry for interrupting your evening."

"No problem at all," smiled Carlos.

"Just for our information, what are you two using this unit for?" asked Pedro, looking round at the empty space.

"Are you making something?"

"We're IT consultants," replied Carlos. "We're just in the process of getting set up."

"Really?" said Pedro looking at the empty table. "I'm sure the landlord said you wanted to start work immediately."

"We just finished one job, and we're waiting for the next," replied Carlos, trying to sound casual.

The officers took another look round the room.

"OK," nodded Carez, "don't forget to call us if you see anything."

"Sure," smiled Carlos. The officers walked out and Carlos shut the door. He motioned for Rudy not to say anything. They waited a full ten minutes before either of them dared to speak.

"Close call," whispered Rudy.

"But nothing more," Carlos reassured him. "They've gone and that's it. Because we said we've seen nothing, they won't bother us again."

"But they'll be back for the bald guy," insisted Rudy.

"That's his problem. Now let's get some sleep. We've still got loads to do tomorrow, OK?"

Rudy nodded, but he was panicked by the police visit. It would be crushing if anything interfered with their plan. But then he reminded himself how near they were to the final stretch. If they could just hold on for a while, it would all come together.

CHAPTER 33
Free Kick Frenzy

In the morning, Inés gave Nat a lift to Talorca's La Plaza Stadium. He'd slept fitfully, with the blackmail-envelope snatch and the Talorca match mixing and frothing in his brain. Today wasn't just massive for him, it was huge for the club. There weren't many teams without silverware and Nat would do anything to make sure Hatton Rangers didn't leave without some. Plus, it would be amazing going into the new season on the back of winning this tournament, especially as five top European teams had competed alongside Hatton Rangers.

The stadium was absolutely incredible – massive and majestic. With a capacity of 60,000, it was only three years old, and the entire structure gleamed in the late morning sunshine. Rangers's home – the Ivy Stadium – was a great structure, but it was old and in need of fundamental repairs. Rangers badly needed to generate more income than at present, if they were to have a chance of even a basic refurbishment. As well as at the Ivy, Nat had played at Anfield, but La Plaza was on another level. It reeked of quality.

The team bus was just pulling away after dropping off its players when Inés's Fiat pulled up. Nat thanked her, jumped out, and caught up with the others. Emi and Kelvin had also just arrived. They all walked through the shimmering glass doors, and were led up an escalator, and along a thickly-carpeted corridor.

"Impressive!" noted Emi, as they took in their new surroundings. The away changing room itself was even better. Tasteful ceiling lights illuminated all of the chrome and glass. The place was spotless and when some of the players went to check out the showers they – particularly Adilson – were taken by their sleek design and the ample bottles of expensive shower gel, shampoo and moisturiser.

"Excuse me if I disappear in there and don't emerge until after the match," said Adilson, miming putting a comb through his hair.

Nat, Emi and Kelvin laughed.

Forty-five minutes later, they followed a long flight of steps downwards and emerged onto the Talorca pitch. It was in pristine condition and several members of the ground staff were standing on the touchline looking at them suspiciously, as if they were planning to drive heavy diggers round their turf and hack it to pieces.

Nat gazed up at the two huge display screens and the towering banks of seats. It was easily as good as any stadium he'd seen anywhere around the world. It might not have the capacity of the Bernabéu or Camp Nou, but it felt equal in stature.

"Gather round!" called Ian Fox. The players sat in a horseshoe shape on the grass. It was another scorching day and several people shielded their eyes from the sun with their hands.

"Well, lads, we've made it," nodded Fox. "We've arrived at a destination this club has never got to before. I can't stress how big a deal this is, particularly for the fans. I know we've enjoyed some promotion campaigns, but we've always achieved that as the second placed team or the team that won in the play-offs. We've never actually brought them any trophies. However, I don't want the weight of expectations crushing you. If we lose, we lose. I'm confident there'll be other finals. But let's try our damnedest to win! You've outplayed Celtic and Lazio. In my opinion, Talorca are no better than either of those teams. Yes, they have home advantage and their fans will scream the place down, but I really think we can brush that aside if we concentrate on our football."

"It would also be beautiful to bring Alberto Tieras down a peg or two!" shouted the Wildman.

Everyone cheered, no one louder than Nat.

"As I outlined," continued Fox, "we're playing four-three-two-one. Some people will think I'm mad to carry out an experiment in such a vital game, but to me it's not an experiment. I can see it working – I can see the finished product. You're the right players for this system."

Nat glanced to his side and saw that Nicky Sinclair's face was pale.

After stretches, runs and drills, Fox separated the

players into position groups. He took all of the midfielders and forwards, while Stan Evans had the defenders. The goalies worked together.

"Now, listen up," said Fox, when he'd taken the eight midfielders and attackers away from the rest of the players. The group consisted of four midfielders – Adilson, Pierre Sacrois, Jermaine Clifton and Luke Summers. The strikers were Jensen, Clarke and Sinclair – all starters – plus Nat.

"There is only one way we're going to score against Talorca tonight, lads, and that's by skill. I genuinely believe we are more technically gifted than they are, and that will mean playing the ball on the ground. Quick passes, one-twos, running at their defenders – if we do all of those things, we will score and we'll have a chance of winning. I particularly want to work on set pieces. We will *not* be lobbing the ball high into their penalty area because there's absolutely no point. Tieras and Co. are phenomenal in the air and will out-jump us nine times out of ten. That's not a criticism of any of you, it's just a fact. If we're not going to outmuscle them, we'll have to out-think them."

All eight players looked at each other and nodded. One thing that could always be said for Ian Fox and Stan Evans, they knew the game backwards and their research on opponents was always impeccable. Their tactical analysis earned the club numerous points each season.

"So the first move to work on relates to if we get a free kick anywhere outside the area, but near enough to cause them damage. I want Adilson to take these free kicks."

Adilson nodded.

"The first free kick we get is going to work like this – Dennis, Robbie and Nicky, I want all of you mixing it up in the penalty area. Swerve, lunge, barge, do anything to give your markers grief. Jermaine, you'll be just inside the area on the right side of the free kick. Talorca won't send out a man to mark you, I'm sure of that. They'll be far more worried about the aggro that's going on in the box. Adilson will take a long run up, suggesting that he's going to whack it in. But . . . he'll strike the ball along the ground to you, Jermaine, and you will shoot immediately. With the curve you can put on a ball, son, you'll be able to get it over their defence and will have a decent chance of scoring. It's nothing revolutionary, but they won't be expecting it."

Nat totally agreed with Fox's idea. It had to be worth having a crack.

"Our second free kick, Adilson will also take. Robbie will be just beside the Talorca wall. When the ball reaches Robbie, he'll flick it with the underside of his boot to Dennis, who will be standing a few yards to the left of the wall. Dennis will then shoot."

"Understood, boss," said Dennis.

"After those first two," added Fox, "I want variations on the same theme – quick free kicks to feet. Short passes and shooting with the minimum of fuss. They'll get our strategy after a few, but hopefully we'll have scored by then. So, Nicky and Nat, go and grab that model wall and bring it over here."

They walked over to the touchline, picked up the model

of a defensive wall with six players painted on its front, and carried it to the others. The next half hour was spent going over these free kicks again and again, involving all eight of them. Nat got plenty of time beside the wall, a few yards away from it, or doing decoy runs. There was a good atmosphere between the players, everyone committed to grabbing a goal at a set play.

Then they hooked up with the others and played some three v three games, and the session ended with seven-a-sides, and then some passing and movement with the eleven who'd be starting. It was nearly 1 p.m. when they finished. Fox and Evans looked satisfied with the session and, as the players filed off the pitch, Nat thought about how much the game meant, not just to the squad, but to Evans and the gaffer. Tonight they could go down in history as the first ever management team to bag a trophy for Hatton Rangers. No wonder they were so fired up.

CHAPTER 34
Inside the Cauldron

Back at the hotel after lunch, the players' visitors started arriving. There were wives and children and cousins and parents – increasing the decibel level in the hotel a hundredfold, as children ran amok in the corridors and squealed with delight in the swimming pool.

Just after two o' clock, Nat saw his father entering the lobby and he ran over to greet him.

"Hi Dad!"

"Nat!" grinned Dave, giving his son a bear hug, which, to Nat's relief, wasn't witnessed by anyone associated with the club.

They sat down at the far side of the lobby and Dave ordered a beer for himself and a coke for his son.

"This is plush!" smiled Dave, taking in his surroundings.

"I know," replied Nat, "but, in a way, it's been better not staying here. It's intense enough spending so much time with the team, so it's good to have a little bolt hole where I can get away from it. Did you bring your harmonica?"

"Damn, I forgot it!" replied Dave in mock horror.

"Excellent!" grinned Nat, who wasn't the number one fan of his dad's music.

"How are you feeling about tonight?"

"I'm nervous, really nervous, even though I'm not in the starting eleven."

"You'll get a decent stint, I reckon," replied Dave.

"We'll see."

"I would love it if you skinned Tieras and scored a sensational goal!"

"Me too!" grinned Nat, who nonetheless shivered at the mere mention of Tieras's name.

"Your mum would have been tickled pink by all of this," said Dave, waving his right arm round at their surroundings. "She was a real outdoors person, she loved camping and nature. But there was a part of her that also loved a bit of luxury. For our fifth wedding anniversary, we stayed for a night at the Landmark Hotel in central London. It was unreal – an amazing room and fantastic service. It was expensive, mind, but totally worth it. We felt like royalty!"

"You must miss her loads," said Nat. "I know I do and I only ever knew her for six years."

"I do, mate," sighed Dave, "I miss her every day. It's weird – it happened over seven years ago, yet I still find myself about to ask her opinion on something or other, and then when I realise she's not here any more, I get a shock."

"Do you think you'll ever . . . you know . . . meet someone else?"

This wasn't something they'd ever really discussed. Over the years, Dave had gone out with a few women, but none of these relationships had ever been serious or lasted long.

"I don't know, Nat, that's the honest answer. Sometimes I think there's no point in even trying, because no one could ever come close to matching your mum. Other times, I tell myself off for being such a fool. Maybe now we're settled back in the UK and we're going to stay put, I might meet someone one day. Never say never."

"You know I wouldn't mind," said Nat. "If you found someone you really liked, I'd have no problem with it."

His dad looked at him with a proud smile on his face. "Thank you," he said, patting his son on the shoulder. "That's an amazing thing to say. If I ever did find someone, I'd only ever let it develop if you liked her. We're in this thing together, and your opinion comes at the top of my list."

They were silent for a minute.

"Do you ever talk about her to any of the other players?" asked Dave.

"It's funny," replied Nat. "I hadn't really until this trip, but then Emi told me his dad was ill back in Ivory Coast, and I spoke to him about Mum. It felt good – you know, it was like a small part of that weight on my shoulders lifted."

"That's good," nodded Dave. "We should both probably talk about her more."

For the next couple of hours, Nat and his father chatted

about everything from their new life back in England, to the rights and wrongs of the formation Ian Fox had opted to play in that night's game. Stan Evans then did the rounds, informing players' guests that visiting time was over. He and Nat's dad shook hands heartily.

"Good to see you, Dave," beamed Evans.

"I'm delighted to be here," replied Dave.

"Well, you should be very proud of your boy. He's done exceptionally well in training and in both substitute appearances he made."

Nat blushed.

"I don't want to embarrass you!" laughed Evans, ruffling Nat's hair. "I'll see you sometime tonight, Dave."

They shook hands again and Evans carried on with his rounds.

"I'm off to my hotel," said Dave. "I'm absolutely whacked. I think I'll do things the Spanish way and have a siesta so I'm fresh for the match."

"Go for it, Dad. And thanks for being here."

"Don't be mad. I wouldn't miss it for the world. I know it's easier said than done, but try not to get too nervous."

They hugged, then Dave walked across the lobby and out of the building.

All round the place, players were saying goodbye to their visitors. There were several outbursts of crying from children who wanted to stay with their dads a bit longer, but within half an hour the hotel was guest-free.

Nat spent the rest of the afternoon on a sunlounger with a large umbrella shading him. He'd found one of the previous day's English newspapers. He started with the sport and worked backwards. When he'd finished with the paper, he grabbed his iPod and spent a while listening to music, dozing and swimming.

By now it was six, and after a light supper it was back onto the team bus. There were already quite a few Talorca supporters in the street outside La Plaza, and they took great pleasure in booing the Rangers coach and making rude gestures at the players. Nat and his teammates laughed.

The bus pulled round the side road beside the stadium and when they'd disembarked, Talorca officials showed them back to the away changing room. In spite of the fact that Stan Evans was circulating, trying to put everyone at their ease, the atmosphere was tense, nervous. Nat saw that the edgiest expressions were on the faces of the older players, including the Wildman. They were well into their careers and this might be their last ever chance of getting their hands on a trophy. When they finally retired from the game, it would be gratifying to look back and see that they'd won at least one final.

Evans led everyone outside onto the pitch for some warm-ups and passing and shooting drills. There was still half an hour until kick off, but the stadium was already three quarters full, and the noise that greeted them was staggering – boos and hisses and angry shouts.

"Blimey," said Kelvin, "these guys take their football seriously."

Nat was also shocked. The crowd noise already sounded

louder than it had at Anfield. The match was going to be an intimidating experience for the Rangers players and they would need to ignore it as best as they could and stick to Ian Fox's game plan.

Back in the changing room, the Wildman started shouting out encouragement.

"We can do this!" he roared, to great yells of approval.

Nat stole a glance at Nicky Sinclair. He'd played in a couple of big games for Aberdeen, but by the look on his face, he was really feeling the pressure of this occasion. His eyes were nervously darting round the room, his body was trembling slightly. Stan Evans saw this too and went over to calm him down. Nat still resented the fact that Fox had gone for Nicky ahead of him, but having heard the boss's rationale behind this, he understood why he'd done it. Maybe he was right. Maybe Tieras would put everything into the match for a while and then lose some of that edge – allowing Fox to send Nat on.

"OK, lads!" shouted Evans, when a Talorca official poked his head round the changing room door and said it was time to move.

The Rangers players shouted to create some positive energy, and emptied out into the tunnel. As usual, Nat hung back with the substitutes. When Talorca FC spilled out, Nat saw that Tieras wasn't with them. Was he injured? Had he been dropped? Nat then spotted their manager, a flamboyant man by the name of Romero Velasquez, go up to Ian Fox and give him a warm handshake. Velasquez hadn't been a great player – he was a bit of a journeyman left-back – but as a manager he'd won La Liga with Sevilla a couple of seasons back and was brimming with confidence. Nat spotted Talorca's playmaker Lombardo up ahead. He was crossing himself and mumbling under his breath.

The sound of the crowd was muted by the walls and ceiling of the tunnel, but it was still very loud. As the referee and his three assistants arrived, Nat saw Tieras emerge from the Talorca changing room and take his place at the head of their line. Tieras turned round, and for a second his and Nat's eyes met. Tieras gave a smug grin. Nat stared back, his body full of loathing.

The referee nodded at his three assistants and they began the walk outside. As the teams emerged into the gleaming floodlights, the noise rose to an almost deafening volume. It made the hairs on the back of Nat's neck stand up. It was a cauldron – bubbling and frothing with passion and soul. The entire stadium was covered in Talorca flags, scarves and banners, and these were joined by huge Spanish flags and placards in Spanish.

Nat spotted the tiny contingent of Hatton Rangers fans, penned into a section of a stand on the far left, doing their very best, but not standing a chance against the overpowering vocal chords of 60,000 home fans.

"This is incredible!" Kelvin shouted at Nat.

The Talorca players were waving to each section of the stadium to acknowledge their devoted following. Nat strolled over to the bench while the two teams stretched alongside each other in two horizontal lines. Victor Mabena and several other dignitaries walked over to shake hands with Tieras. The Talorca captain introduced Mabena and crew to his players. It was then the turn of the Wildman to press flesh with Mabena and the dignitaries before introducing them to the Rangers players. This done, the two teams shook each other's hands and sprinted off, Talorca to the home end, Rangers to the away end – which was like another home end because it was so jam-packed with Talorca fans.

The Rangers players were met by a huge wall of sound – a cascading outpouring of boos. They did their best to ignore it, but it was loud and hostile, and it would take a robot to be able to fully block it out.

The game hadn't started, but Ian Fox was already at the far edge of his technical area, screaming out instructions to his players.

"Kelvin, look out for Raymond Hilva, he looks like he's back to full fitness!"

Hilva was their bulky centre-forward. He was fast and very agile.

"Clarke, don't stray too far from Jensen!"

The Rangers manager was wringing his hands together and looking as if he was letting his players loose in the world's most dangerous combat zone.

"Adilson, don't forget the first free kick!" yelled Stan Evans.

Nat studied Alberto Tieras. Even though he was further away from Nat than he'd been at the radio studio, he actually looked bigger out on the pitch. He was a massive brute of a man – someone who had unshakeable belief in himself and his own powers, particularly here, in his home stadium. The Talorca supporters shared this belief. Tieras was their talisman, the man who won games by his single-mindedness. He played the same sort of role as the Wildman did for Rangers. Every team needed someone like that – a fearless player, who would put his head where others wouldn't put their feet.

Nat felt his own feet jiggling up and down with nerves.

The referee checked with his assistants, looked at his watch and blew his whistle.

CHAPTER 35
A Crushing Blow

Talorca had kick off and the Rangers players were shocked at the instant aggressive force of their opponents' attack. Inside the first minute. Talorca could have scored. Hilva's shot swept just over the bar of Graham Dalston's goal. This acted as a severe warning, but Rangers could hardly get hold of the ball. It was all Talorca, and before ten minutes were up, they'd forced two superb saves from Dalston and hit the post.

Ian Fox was apoplectic, shrieking at his players to get the ball, keep it on the ground and *retain* it. But however hard the Hatton Rangers players tried, Talorca enjoyed the lion's share of possession. It was as though they were taunting Rangers.

And then, in the fifteenth minute, Adilson wrestled the ball from their right-sided midfielder Andres Luerta, and ran down the left touchline. He cut in and feigned shooting, before sliding the ball to Nicky Sinclair. Sinclair was right on the cusp of the penalty area and he'd just controlled the ball when he was hacked down by Tieras.

"PENALTY!" screamed every person in the stadium

who was connected to Hatton Rangers. The Rangers players swarmed over to the referee. It was a textbook foul. A penalty and a booking had to be the immediate response. But the referee disagreed with all of them and gave Rangers a free kick on the edge of the penalty area. And his yellow card stayed inside his pocket.

"You must be joking!" shrieked Ian Fox in rage. "It was a clear penalty!"

The referee was unmoved by any of the protests and ushered the Rangers players away. Nat shook his head in disbelief and watched Adilson place the ball and then hold a brief discussion with Jermaine Clifton. This was Rangers's first free kick. They were going to follow Fox's precise instructions.

Nat was totally caught in the moment. Would Adilson and Jermaine Clifton deliver? Adilson stood over the ball. Clifton took up a position just inside the penalty area, as Fox had instructed, to Adilson's right. Xavier Bergas in the Talorca goal was yelling at his players, who were forming a defensive wall. Jensen, Clarke and Nicky Sinclair were also doing as Fox had told them. They were jostling, pushing and barging into the Talorca wall, causing the Talorca players all sorts of trouble. Tieras was screaming at the Hatton Rangers trio of interlopers, but they ignored him and maximised their interference with Talorca's defensive plans.

Nat smiled. *Put it away, Jermaine!*

The Talorca left-back Henry Paret spotted Clifton, hesitated for a moment and then started running over to mark him. Nat tensed, but Tieras shouted at Paret to come back and make up the numbers in the wall.

Jermaine Clifton was on his own – just like the gaffer had said he'd be.

Adilson took about ten steps back to increase the impression that he was going to smack the ball high and hard into the box. Bergas was squinting to check his wall was in the optimum position. Tieras was clapping his hands and shouting at his teammates. As soon as the referee blew, Adilson ran speedily towards the ball and for a moment it looked like he really was going to smash it in.

It was a brilliant piece of football theatre. As his foot connected with the ball, the Talorca players in the wall jumped to intercept his rocket, but were stunned mid-jump to see Adilson hit it straight along the ground to Clifton.

Clifton hit it first time – a beautiful, powerful bullet that curved right round the wall and hurtled goalwards. Bergas was unsighted, but instinct forced him to leap. He flew across his goal as the ball smashed towards the net. His fingertips just managed to reach it and push it round the post for a corner.

No!

Ian Fox and Stan Evans were on their feet, convinced the ball was going in, and both threw their arms up in frustration when Bergas saved it. It wasn't a goal, but the Rangers players had followed Ian Fox's instructions to the letter, and Nat could see that, despite his disappointment, the boss was pleased with them.

Tieras was shrieking at his players for letting Jermaine Clifton in, forgetting it was *him* who'd ordered Paret not to mark Clifton. In the next five minutes, Talorca mounted two good attacks, one ending with a very good dive, parry and then catch by Dalston.

On twenty minutes, Nicky Sinclair picked up the ball just inside the Rangers half. Even though Robbie Clarke was yelling for the ball on the right wing, Sinclair went for the more cautious option and passed the ball back in the direction of the Wildman. But he didn't get enough power on the ball and it trickled well short of the Rangers captain. The Wildman instantly spotted the mistake and made a dash for the ball, but Lombardo was faster and he sprinted in, took the ball round the Wildman and released Raymond Hilva. Hilva sold a dummy to the onrushing Kelvin, rounded Dalston and smacked the ball home.

One-nil to Talorca.

Nicky Sinclair's mistake had been a schoolboy one and he sank to his knees, head in hands. It wasn't even the halfway point of the first half yet, but he realised his slip might have just cost Hatton Rangers their first ever trophy.

The Wildman ran straight over to Sinclair, pulled him to his feet and put an arm round his shoulders. Sinclair's eyes were red and watery. Nat looked sideways and saw Ian Fox and Stan Evans staring at Sinclair with disbelief. Graham Dalston angrily fetched the ball from his net and booted it back to the halfway line. Adilson trapped it and placed it on the centre circle, ready for kick off. On the whistle, he passed it to Sacrois who fed it on to Sinclair. But Sinclair panicked and whacked the ball up-field and into touch.

Ian Fox was instantly on his feet.

"Get your tracksuit off!" he commanded at Nat. "I can't leave Sinclair on!"

The match was twenty-two minutes old.

I'm coming on in the first half for the first time!

Nat felt terrible for Nicky, but this was his chance to grab a much larger slice of a game than he'd ever expected, and he wasn't going to waste it. His tracksuit top and trousers were off in a second and he was stretching and jumping on the touchline. Fox quickly notified the fourth official who nodded and started tapping the info into his scoreboard.

"It's going to be very tough for Nicky," Stan Evans shouted at Nat, "but we can't leave him out there. It will only make things worse. We don't want to get into a situation where he keeps on making mistakes. Our fans will start booing him and that's a very hard thing to recover from. Nat, you're to play on the right, tucking in just behind Jensen, OK?"

Nat nodded and took another couple of jumps. It was time to see if Tieras would make good his promise to put Nat on a stretcher. Part of Nat felt a deep, cold fear. After all, Tieras was a monster of a man. But another part of him relished the challenge. Tieras had used his mouth to attack Rangers and him personally over the course of the last few days, but it was what happened out on the pitch that counted, and Nat was going to bust every sinew he possessed to get one over on the Talorca captain.

"Look out for Tieras," said Ian Fox, the mind-reader, placing a hand on Nat's back. "But remember, everyone is watching him and if he crosses the line we'll all be on to him. You're quicker than him, you're cleverer than him. We're not expecting you to carry all of our hopes on your shoulders but we know what you can do."

On the pitch, Adilson hit a long, raking pass towards Robbie Clarke. But he over-hit and it went out on the far touchline. The fourth official immediately held up his board. Nicky Sinclair saw his number and his face crumpled. On the basis of the way he was playing, it made sense to withdraw him but it didn't stop him feeling totally crushed. He shuffled dejectedly off the pitch like someone sixty years his senior. When he reached the touchline, he shook Nat's hand and mouthed, "Good luck," before going straight into the tunnel.

The fourth assistant checked Nat's boots and he was on.

Coming on as a substitute against Manchester United had been utterly incredible, but somehow this felt like a bigger occasion because of the silverware available – the thing every fan dreamed about.

Nat ran straight into position – on the right, playing behind Dennis Jensen, with Robbie Clarke performing the same role on the left. Within three minutes of being on, Nat combined well with Clarke and hit the ball to Adilson, who smashed in a volley that just missed the bar.

Tieras was furious with his defenders for letting Adilson through and yelled at them, presumably ordering them to go on the offensive, because what happened next was more like Tieras's battlefield than a game of football. With the exception of Tieras, every Talorca player rushed forwards, determined that by sheer numbers alone they'd bag a goal.

Lombardo was suddenly on fire. He cruised past the Rangers defenders as if they were mannequins, and had three excellent efforts in a blazing seven minute period. Remarkably, however, the match stayed one-nil, thanks to some heroic defending by the Hatton Rangers back four, particularly Emi.

But the head of steam Talorca had built up convinced them they would score again and their assault continued. So instead of seeing action in the Talorca half, Nat found himself back in the Hatton Rangers area, defending with everyone else. He got in a particularly good tackle on Paret that denied the Talorca player a good shooting chance.

Towards the end of the half, Adilson managed to get the ball off Talorca and made a break down the left flank. Nat, Clarke and Jensen hared up the pitch towards the penalty area. Adilson squared the ball to Dennis Jensen in the D. Jensen could have shot, but he stroked it on to Clarke, who rounded Tieras and slipped the ball to Nat.

Nat struck it first time, low and hard. He watched it fly goalwards and his heart leapt. It was going in! He was going to square the game for Rangers! But Bergas, who looked well beaten, lunged for the ball and just managed to get his right boot to it. His touch pushed it onto the post and off the field for a corner.

I can't believe that didn't go in!

Before Rangers could get the ball to the corner flag, the referee blew for half-time. Fox and Evans were instantly on their feet, shouting at the referee and pointing to their watches. In their minds, there was still a minute of time added on, but he ignored them and motioned for the players to vacate the pitch.

Nat felt a huge burst of deflation over his near miss. But Emi ran over to him and shouted, "That was a brilliant move!"

The mood in the changing room was relatively calm, but everyone had been pushed by the relentlessness of the Talorca attacks. They'd spent a huge part of the first half pinned back in their penalty area in a desperate effort to keep the ball out. Everyone noticed that Nicky Sinclair wasn't around.

"The ref blew too early!" was Fox's opening gambit. His face was lit up with passion and determination. "And that last move was spot on, lads! We have the beating of Talorca within us. More attacking moves like that and we'll score. Yes, they had massive chunks of possession and they're one-nil up. But you defended brilliantly – that goes for the forwards and midfielders as well as our defence. It was a good team effort. In the second half, we'll put the cat among the pigeons and spring at them. Let's shock those Talorca players and their fans! Do you get what I'm saying?"

"Yes, boss!" chorused the players.

Coming out for the second half, Nat and the Rangers players felt much more upbeat, spurred on by Fox's words. The manager had praised both the team's attacking and defending. That was something!

But Fox's plans for Rangers to put their opponents onto the back foot didn't materialise. Talorca came out with a swagger and once again kept the ball to themselves. Their fans loved it, cheering every pass.

Nat looked around. He and the Rangers players were in danger of becoming so frustrated that they'd do anything to get the ball back. The sixty minute mark passed without a single Rangers shot. On sixty-three minutes, Lombardo tried an audacious punt from fifty yards that Dalston had to stretch for. Talorca were starting to mock Rangers and parade their superiority with a palpable arrogance.

The Rangers players were getting wound up, and Nat could feel the tension buzzing inside him. He couldn't stand the stifling way Talorca were running the game. So he decided to do something about it. Luerta was standing near Rangers's right-hand corner flag, so Nat sprinted over, bustled the Talorca player and stole the ball from him. He then flicked the ball through his legs. Luerta pulled Nat's shirt but Nat shoulder-barged him away.

Then he was off. Nat saw the whole pitch in front of him, the long shadows like extended fingers cutting over the turf. Running at pace, but keeping the ball close to him, he took it round Raymond Hilva. Henry Paret came charging forwards to stop him. Nat made as if he was going to go left, then dropped his shoulder and went right. Paret got a foot to the ball but it wasn't enough to dispossess Nat.

It was then that Nat became aware of Emi, who had run the entire length of the pitch, and was now parallel with him. Emi was steaming into the Talorca box, screaming for the ball, with Alberto Tieras in close proximity. Nat took the ball right to the byeline and hit a beautifully weighted pass straight to Emi.

Emi controlled it on his chest, spun away from Tieras and shot. It was an exquisite piece of skill for a defender.

The ball dipped and crashed past Bergas into the Talorca goal.

Nat was instantly yelling and running towards Emi. The rest of the Rangers players weren't far behind and in a few seconds Emi was completely smothered by teammates.

But then Nat heard the referee's whistle. He turned and saw the ref pointing to his hand for a free kick to Talorca. There was no flag from the nearest assistant referee, but the referee was in no doubt. In his view, Emi had handled the ball. The goal had been disallowed.

was a free kick to Talorca because of Emi's 'handball', and that both teams had to regroup at once. He wasn't going to be having any conversations about the incident. It wasn't a goal – his decision was final. If anyone kept berating him, then he'd yellow or red card them, if necessary.

The Wildman could see there was nothing that could be done to get the referee to alter his stance, so, with great reluctance and a feeling of despair, he shepherded Emi and the rest of the players away from the referee. Nat saw that, as well as the hysteria from the crowd, Tieras and several of the other Talorca players were laughing.

Talk about twisting the knife!

But then the match took a hateful twist. As Emi shook his head in despair and started trudging back up the pitch, a banana hit the touchline nearest to him. Nat stared in shock at the section of the crowd it had been thrown from. And then more bananas came flying onto the touchline, with several landing on the pitch. Within seconds, the same section of Talorca fans started making monkey noises.

Nat was staggered. He'd heard about the abuse black players had endured in the seventies and eighties in England, but he was well aware of the changes that had taken place in recent years. Let's Kick Racism Out of Football and other high profile campaigns had let racists know they had no place in football. There were numbers to text or call if you spotted anyone shouting racist abuse in the stands. Then stewards and the police got to these people very quickly and they were not only booted out of the stadium, but some were arrested, convicted and banned for life from attending football matches. The Premier League was now largely shorn of these repulsive people, although there were still problems with racist chanting in some of the lower leagues.

But this was Talorca FC – a La Liga One team, a team that regularly played Champions League football across the continent. Nat span round and looked at the nearest huddle of police officers. None of them were making a move towards the fans behind this sickening spectacle.

Emi looked at this section of the stadium with disgust. The Wildman raced over to the referee and pointed out what was happening. The referee blew his whistle and signalled to the Talorca stewards to remove the bananas from the pitch, which they did. Nat could see that when the bananas had been removed the referee was going to wave play on, even though the chanting and noises continued. Rage pumped through Nat's veins and he could see the same fury on Emi's face and on those of his teammates. Nat and Emi sprinted across to the referee to join the Wildman.

"We must play on," the referee was telling the Wildman. "The problem is over."

"No it isn't!" shouted Nat. "Just listen!"

The noises were coming from the same small band of supporters, but it was getting louder.

"This is the twenty-first century!" shouted Emi. "We're not standing for it!"

"Too right!" snarled the Wildman. "They go or we do!"

The referee hesitated, unsure what to do.

And then Tieras strolled up, a big grin on his face. "Frightened, are we?" he shouted. "Frightened of a few supporters?"

"It's not about being frightened!" snarled the Wildman, facing up to him. "It's about that scum over there – what they threw and what they're shouting!"

"If you can't take it, you shouldn't be a footballer!" sneered Tieras.

"That's pathetic!" shouted Nat. "They're *your* supporters, *you* should do something about them!"

But Tieras shook his head with contempt. "Play or lose the match!" he snapped.

By this point, the chanting had risen another few decibels, with the police and the referee doing nothing. The Wildman had seen and heard enough.

"We're out of here!" he shouted, gesturing with his arms for his teammates to follow him. They did this to a man, and a moment later, all eleven of them were marching towards the touchline. As they walked, the overwhelming majority of the rest of the Talorca fans and all of the Rangers fans got to their feet and applauded them. It was a rapturous swirl of noise and completely drowned out the chants of the racists.

Thank God those idiots are a tiny minority!

As this crescendo of crowd noise rose, Raymond Hilva, Xavier Bergas, Henry Paret, Nicolas Sorin and Leo Gallant from the Talorca team walked off too.

Ian Fox, Stan Evans and the Talorca manager Velasquez

stood by the touchline, their hands held aloft to applaud all of their players who were striding off the pitch.

The referee, seeing he'd been heavily outvoted by this marching group of players, ran over to consult his assistants. The two of them had a quick consversation with some club officials and senior police officers and a minute later, a large group of policemen in full riot gear appeared and started running towards the offending section of the crowd. Without hesitation, they steamed in, and although they were met by punches and kicks, they took less than three minutes to grab the troublemakers, pull them out of the stand and drag them along the touchline, where they were met by the sounds of tens of thousands of fans booing and heckling them.

Nat looked back to the pitch, where the only players remaining were Tieras and five of his teammates. Tieras's face was filled with utter disgust. Nat could only imagine the confrontation he'd have with his other five colleagues later.

When all of the troublemakers had been led away and the sound of their chanting had completely stopped, the referee blew his whistle for the sixteen protesting players to return to the pitch. As they re-entered the field of play, the applause and cheering rose even louder.

Tieras watched his returning players with contempt, but there were five of them, and he couldn't take them all on in one go. The referee called Tieras and the Wildman over for a drop ball to restart the game. Tieras got his foot in first and whacked it to Paret. Hatton Rangers had less

CHAPTER 36
A Despicable Act

The Talorca fans went crazy, celebrating as if they'd just won the game.

Nat was stunned. He'd had a clear view of Emi's excellent trap and shot. The ball hadn't touched his arm or hand at all – not even slightly. As the referee's decision filtered through to the other Rangers players, they turned and pelted towards him. The Talorca fans were still screaming with delight.

"You've got to be joking!" roared Emi at the front of the pack, his face lit up with rage.

"It was a clear goal!" added a seething Nat.

Suddenly Tieras was there. He grabbed Emi's arm and pulled him away from the melee to remonstrate with him.

"No goal!" he shouted in Emi's face.

Emi responded furiously, shoving Tieras in the chest and screaming back, "I didn't touch it with my hand!"

Several other Talorca players now ran to this hotspot like moths to candlelight. The referee was quick to get between the two sets of players, instructing them that it

CHAPTER 37
Perfect Strikes

With such an unpleasant incident marring the game, all of
the Talorca players, and especially Alberto Tieras, would
be wanting to end the match on a high by holding their
lead or increasing it.

Talorca had clearly been instructed to up their tempo
in search of a second and match-finishing goal. This they
did with gusto, and Lombardo, in particular, improved
his game, passing Rangers players with flicks and
twists and step-overs, and going close twice – once with
a volley from inside the box that skimmed the bar, and
the other time with a header that Dalston leaped for
and caught.

The eightieth minute mark passed and, with Talorca
piling players forward, it seemed their momentum would
yield that second goal. But on eighty-two minutes, from a
Dalston throw-out, a Rangers attack began to build. Kelvin
Bartlett received the ball in the right-back position and
fed it cross-field to Andy Young on the left. Young pushed
it towards Adilson, who was hugging the left touchline.

With his first touch, Adilson stopped the ball; with

his second he whacked it to Nat, who was cross-pitch on the right. Nat controlled the ball with his right instep. As Raymond Hilvas dived in to grab the ball, Nat pushed it round him. Hilvas hit the turf and Nat was gone.

Up ahead of him, he could see Jensen and Clarke pounding into the penalty area, and he thought about immediately passing to one of them. But they were both being closely marked, and if Nat could beat the approaching Henry Paret, he'd have a scoring chance. Paret was speeding towards him with steely determination rippling over his face. Nat waited until Paret was almost on him, before suddenly accelerating to Paret's right and flicking the ball ahead of him. Paret stretched to reach it, but it was just beyond him.

Nat was now on the right side edge of the penalty area, and he saw that Clarke had ducked away from his marker and was shouting for the ball. He made a split-second decision and Clarke lost out. Entering the penalty area, Nat spotted Xavier Bergas slightly off his line, and, feigning a pass, he floated an outrageous lob with the outside of his right boot towards the Talorca goal. For a moment it looked like he'd over-hit it, and that it would just miss the crossbar. But at the crucial second, it dipped and, despite Bergas's terrific leap, it rose over his body and into the Talorca net.

It was an incredible goal, and in a second Nat had the entire Rangers team leaping on his back, pummelling their fists into him. He listened out for the referee's whistle – would the ref disallow another perfectly legitimate

England, the hard work will begin. Now thank you, ladies and gentlemen, I have a squad to celebrate with."

And with that, he swept out of the room. Stan Evans switched off the TV and the singing, led by the Wildman, started up all over again. A few minutes later, Fox returned to the changing room and went round to every player shaking their hands and thanking them.

"Well done, Nat," he said, with a firm handshake. "They were both good goals."

That was it, but it meant a lot to Nat.

It took over an hour before the players were all sung out, and, clutching the trophy tightly, the Wildman led everyone outside. The players' families were waiting by the team bus and they let out deafening rounds of cheers and applause. The wives, girlfriends and children mobbed them. In the melee, Nat was grabbed by his jubilant father.

"Nat – you were magnificent!"

"Cheers, Dad."

"It was an outstanding performance, Nat. The second goal was a peach. I am SO proud of you!"

"It was great to be out there and score. The sound was incredible. It made the Ivy Stadium feel like a school playground!"

"Well, Ian Fox can only be pleased with you. You've got to keep working hard for him and the team, and who knows what will happen."

"Shall I meet you before Mabena's lunch thing tomorrow?"

Rangers goal? But he just blew for a Talorca restart. The goal stood.

"You little beauty!" shouted the Wildman.

"I cannot believe you just did that!" laughed Emi deliriously.

Nat broke away from the players and ran over to the Hatton Rangers supporters. They were going mad with exhilaration, their voices chorusing his name over and over. He kissed the Rangers badge on his shirt and leapt into the air, punching his right fist skywards as he did so. Tieras and the Talorca team looked taken aback, as if it was an affront to football etiquette for these English minnows to score against such Spanish might.

"Fantastic!" grinned Robbie Clarke, hugging Nat. "For a second I was furious with you because I was in a decent spot and I thought you were going to pass to me, but you did the right thing! How good was it to see Xavier Bergas tipping backwards in panic as the ball sailed over his head? Great goal, mate!"

Talorca one, Hatton Rangers one.

The referee broke the spell of crazed celebration and shouted at the Rangers players to get back into their own half. Bergas kicked the ball in disgust to the halfway line and Talorca prepared for a centre. The Wildman marshalled his troops back into shape.

Tieras ran up the pitch to take the centre. He stroked it to Hilva who hit it back to him. The Talorca captain was clearly determined to take the match by the scruff of the neck and impose his will upon it – taking on the entire for his father's death and the termination of his own football career.

No wonder José hated Mabena. No wonder he wanted to steal the man's car. It wasn't much – Mabena could easily afford a new car – but it was a finger in the eye. It would inconvenience and probably infuriate the Talorca President – his car being stolen from the safety of his team's supposedly 'secure' stadium executive car park.

Nat carried on searching for more information. Everything he found mirrored the first article. Some people blamed Mabena and his company for the crashes, others said they were simply down to drivers losing concentration, or, in one article, possibly falling asleep at the wheel. After a long official enquiry, the court passed a verdict of accidental death in the case of Frederico Mancini.

When Nat finally flipped the laptop shut, he checked his watch and saw it was 12.53. Mabena's lunch started at 1 p.m. Nat was going to be pretty late for it, especially as he was going to have to walk down to the main road to catch the bus to La Plaza Stadium. But there would probably be loads of glad-handing and chat before the meal. No doubt he had far more time than he thought.

So he didn't rush his shower. When he'd finished, it was 1.25 p.m. He knelt down by the trousers he'd worn the night before to get his ID pass for La Plaza Stadium. But he couldn't find it. He quickly checked the other pockets, but without luck. He looked in his wallet and his bag, and then under the bed and all over his bedroom floor.

Rangers team by himself if that was what was required. If the match was a draw, extra time would follow, and if the stalemate persisted, it would go to a penalty shoot-out. Tieras wanted to win it within the ninety minutes plus any stoppage time.

Tieras's first attempt to smash down the pitch was halted by a brilliant tackle by Emi, who also managed to boot the ball up-field to Clarke and then run onwards. But Clarke's pass to Jensen was intercepted by Henry Paret, who hit it back into the Rangers half, where Lombardo controlled it and then flicked it on to Tieras – now waiting menacingly just outside the penalty area.

Tieras entered the Rangers box, but the Wildman was waiting for him. Tieras dribbled the ball straight in the Wildman's direction. The Wildman stood firm and their shoulders clashed with a mighty thud. The ball rolled towards Kelvin. But Tieras wasn't finished. He elbowed the Wildman in the chest and ran after the ball. The Wildman winced and then squared up to Tieras.

"Can't stand being tackled fairly, can you?" yelled the Wildman.

"You foul *me*," bellowed Tieras.

"Rubbish!" countered the Wildman.

The two of them stood there, nose to nose, fury and hatred scorching their faces. Tieras then gave the Wildman a much stronger and more aggressive shove in the chest. The Wildman stood his ground and didn't attack back. This only served to further incense Tieras and he aimed a punch at the Wildman's head. But the Wildman ducked and Tieras nearly fell over. Before he could swing again, the referee was there, standing resolutely between the two captains.

"Back off!" commanded the referee.

"Willingly," said the Wildman.

But Tieras's rage was out of control, and in a fit of sheer madness he took a swipe at the referee. The blow hit him hard on the shoulder and the referee went crashing onto the ground.

"What the hell are you doing?" shouted the Wildman, giving the very shaken referee a hand to get back to his feet.

The referee reached into his pocket and instantly produced a red card, which he held right in Tieras's face.

"Get off!" commanded the referee furiously. "NOW!"

Tieras stood quite still, looking in stunned silence at the red card.

"You heard the man!" cried the Wildman.

"OFF. NOW!" repeated the ref.

Tieras shook his head violently, and it looked as though he might attack the referee again, or anyone else in the vicinity, but then he turned and stormed off the pitch, chucking the captain's armband to Henry Paret. As he reached the touchline, his manager tried to put an arm round him, but Tieras flung it away and disappeared into the tunnel.

The referee indicated for a Rangers free kick on the spot where Tieras had shoved the Wildman. Emi took it and released Jermaine Clifton, but his run was blocked by

Talorca. There followed a short period of possession for both sides. It wasn't long before Stan Evans was holding up one finger to indicate that the match had just entered its eighty-ninth minute.

The fourth official held up his board to show that there would be five minutes of time added on. Nat looked around at his teammates and the Talorca players. It was clear that the Spanish players were less exhausted than the English crew. They were used to the local climate. Nat and the Rangers team were tiring badly. If they didn't grab something in the five minutes of added time, they'd be sure to fade in the half an hour of extra time, and that only pointed to one thing – a Talorca victory.

I have to do something!

Two minutes into the added time, Nat exchanged a couple of passes with Emi, but the ball eventually hit Adilson and went out for a throw-in to Talorca.

But Paret fluffed the throw. Adilson ran on to the ball and sprinted into the Talorca half. Nat started running towards the penalty area, with Robbie Clarke and Dennis Jensen just ahead of him. Adilson swerved past the onrushing Lombardo. He cut inside and looked up.

Nat, Jensen and Clarke were in the penalty area now, all yelling for the ball. Raymond Hilva, Henry Paret and Leo Gallant were shadowing them. But as the ball left Adilson's boot, a sudden revelation hit Nat. Although Adilson's play could be wildly unorthodox and, at times, surreal, Nat had had ample chances to study his crossing. And he knew this one would go to the far right edge of the penalty area. So, as Clarke and Jensen prepared to jump alongside Hilva and Paret, Nat darted rightwards, leaving his marker, Leo Gallant, a few paces away from him.

The cross was a beauty and, just as Nat had predicted, it rose over the heads of the others. It cleared Leo Gallant, whose jump was a few centimetres short. This left Nat, unmarked, with the ball heading straight for him. He knew instantly how he was going to hit it. He needed to be fast and forceful. As the ball descended, Nat lent back and hit it on the volley, high, and with his right foot.

His connection was excellent and he watched as the ball flew towards the Talorca goal. Bergas was clearly sighted and he flung himself to catch it. But it was moving too fast and he couldn't quite get his fingertips to it. The ball scraped the inside of the post and flew forcefully into the back of the net.

The next few seconds were completely crazy. If his teammates had been delighted with his first goal, they were delirious over his second. He was buried beneath a great mass of leaping and screaming Hatton Rangers players. The referee was quickly at their side, yelling at them to get up and let the centre be taken. The game wasn't over yet.

Nat stood, his face covered in mud, as well as the front of his shirt, shorts and knees. He'd just scored a brace of goals in the final of a tournament, and if Rangers could hang on to their lead for just two minutes, the trophy would be theirs!

The Talorca players looked even more stunned than

before, but Lombardo managed to retrieve the ball and he raced towards the centre circle. He took the kick quickly, hit it to Gallant, who passed it straight back. Lombardo then went on an amazing twisting run, rounding three Rangers players, before entering the penalty area. He dragged his right foot back to hit it, but, before he made another contact with the ball, the Wildman slid in with one of his trademark last-gasp tackles.

As the ball skimmed towards Kelvin Bartlett, the Talorca players and fans shrieked for a penalty. Nat stared in fear at the referee for an agonising few seconds, but the referee ignored all the pleas and waved play on. Kelvin ran up the right flank, with no Talorca players anywhere near him. His destination was the right corner flag. There he could shield the ball as the seconds counted down to the full-time whistle.

But Lombardo raced across and dispossessed him. Nat groaned. Another Lombardo attack could result in the goal Talorca needed. Kelvin tracked back and managed to prise the ball away from Lombardo. He then booted it out for a Talorca throw-in.

Hilva screamed at a ball boy for the ball, but as his throw floated through the air, the referee blew his whistle.

The match was over!

CHAPTER 38
Silverware at Last

Talorca FC one, Hatton Rangers two.

Nat Dixon's two goals had just won Hatton Rangers their first piece of silverware in the club's history!

The stunned Talorca players either sat down on the pitch or stumbled over to the touchline. They couldn't believe what had happened. They'd presumed before the match that the trophy was theirs, but they'd ended up with nothing.

The Rangers players hugged each other, jumped in the air and danced. Then they raced towards their supporters for a few minutes of screaming and cheering.

"One Nat Dixon, there's only one Nat Dixon!" sang the fans. Nat waved gratefully to them, his mind exploding with joy.

Whatever happens in the future, I'll always have this night to remember – so I've got to live in the minute!

"Over here, boys!" The Rangers's players delirious cavorting was interrupted by their manager. "COME ON!" hollered Fox.

They turned round and saw that a long platform had

man's grasp. At that second, he spotted a tiny switch on the underside of the panel.

Four, three, two. . .

Nat pressed the switch as hard as he could, waiting for the blast below. But the digital countdown stopped. On one second.

The switch must be an override button. If he hadn't pressed it, carnage would have ensued. Nat staggered to his feet and looked out of the window. The back lights glowed on Mabena's car and the driver eased it out of the parking space.

José and the other man were both on the ground, moaning like wounded animals. The door swung open and Nat's father strode into the room. He looked at the two prostrate bodies and at the black panel his son was holding.

"Nat," gaped Dave, "what the hell's going on? Where have you been?"

"How did you know I was here?" panted Nat.

"Well, you didn't show up at the lunch," replied Dave, staring at the moaning figures lying on the floor, "so I was worried about you. And you weren't answering your mobile. Kelvin saw you at the door, looking into the banqueting hall, and told me. So I went out to find you and saw you disappearing into the lift. I called your name but you ran in. When I made it to the lift I saw from the display that you'd gone to the fifth floor. I pressed and pressed to recall the lift but it didn't come so I took the stairs. I heard some sort of commotion coming from in been set up near the tunnel and that the Talorca players were already walking along it, shaking hands with club chairman Victor Mabena, and accepting their runners-up medals, their heads held low with disappointment and shame. They waited for the Rangers players to approach them and then shook all of their hands, gracious in defeat. Lombardo took off his shirt and walked over to Nat. Nat took off his and they exchanged.

"You have a big future," smiled Lombardo. "I wish you much luck."

"Thanks!" grinned Nat, putting on Lombardo's top.

The Talorca players then walked over to the tunnel, understandably not wanting to hang around to see Hatton Rangers receiving the trophy. Several of the other Rangers players had swapped shirts and the excitement crackled among them as the Wildman started walking towards the presentation table.

Victor Mabena, whose team had just lost the final, was also warm in defeat. Nat was fifth in line after the Wildman, Emi, Kelvin and Dennis Jensen. Mabena indicated for the players to approach him. The Wildman stepped forward and shook hands with the Talorca president, who placed a medal round his neck.

Mabena paused for a second, looked wistfully at the trophy, then picked it up and handed it to the Wildman. The captain, a man totally committed to the 'whole team' ethic, did not raise the trophy aloft yet. He would only do that when all of his teammates had received their medals. So he walked to the end of the platform and waited.

Nat watched Emi, Kelvin and Jensen receive their medals from Mabena. Then it was his turn.

Those eight or nine steps felt as dramatic as a moonwalk for Nat and it seemed to take him forever to get there. But suddenly Mabena was shaking his hand and placing a gold medal on a white and blue chord around his neck.

"Very well played, young man!" said the Talorca President. "It's always good to see new talent coming through. Both goals were beautiful!"

Nat thanked him and walked over to the others. It was a well thought out presentation because each of the Rangers substitutes also received a medal, saving them from that bizarre situation of celebrating a trophy with no medal, even if they'd appeared in the group games.

When everyone was through, the Wildman and his players turned to face their shrieking band of supporters, and the Hatton Rangers captain lifted the trophy high above his head. The supporters roared with joy and the Wildman, eager to share the spoils, passed the trophy to Emi. As he lifted it up, the fans yelled again. Emi knew exactly who he was going to hand the trophy on to – he quickly passed it to Nat.

Nat held the handles of the beautiful silver prize and raised it as high as he could. The fans yelled his name and they were joined by his teammates. In many ways, this was Nat's hour.

The rest of the players each took a turn lifting the trophy and then it was time to run over to their supporters to parade their historic first. Ian Fox and Stan Evans – who'd also won medals – accompanied them, although their celebrations were more muted than that of their players.

Nat's immense joy was suddenly tempered as he thought of how much his mum would have loved to have seen this moment – out on a Spanish pitch, the hero of a trophy-winning performance.

But as the fans' voices grew even louder and the players jumped over the barrier surrounding the pitch and went right up to them, Nat told himself again to enjoy the moment.

The supporters reached out to shake hands with as many of the players as possible. Nat's hand was shaken at least a hundred times, his hair was ruffled constantly and one older supporter even managed to squeeze his cheek.

Lots of fans also got a chance to touch the trophy, as the Wildman, in extravagantly generous spirits, held it out to them. Fans also placed Rangers hats on the players' heads and scarves round their necks. Nat soon had three hats balancing precariously on top of his head.

With one last round of handshakes and mutual congratulations, the players stepped back over the barrier, gave their fans one last wave and began the walk back towards the tunnel. A couple of photographers made them stop for team photos, which they posed for with pleasure.

Andy Young had the cup now and he was dancing and swinging it above his head, an act that made Nat and everyone else laugh crazily. He looked like Nobby Stiles had done after England won the World Cup in 1966.

The Wildman ran over to Nat and gave him a playful punch on the arm.

"Nat Dixon!" he cried. "What the hell would we do without you? You saved our skins against Man United and now you produce two acts of wizardry! Are you human?"

"It was a team effort!" protested Nat. "Everyone got stuck in!"

"You're right about that," agreed the Wildman, "but every great team is built around one special player."

Nat felt a brittle lump in his throat at these words, but then Emi leapt onto his back and placed a fourth Rangers hat on top of his already teetering pile. Nat whacked Emi with the Rangers scarf he'd been given.

The joyous party walked down towards the tunnel and Nat took one last look around the stadium. It was rapidly emptying, but the Hatton Rangers fans remained, singing at the tops of their voices. Nat scanned the huge stands and the powerful floodlight beams, savouring the sights, smells and noises. He then dragged his eyes away and followed his teammates into the tunnel, their studs echoing on the concrete floor, their spirits probably higher than those of any Hatton Rangers players in the club's history.

In the changing room, there was singing, conga lines, chanting, back-slapping and general merriment, which was louder and more raucous than anything Nat had experienced before.

"We've won the cup!" sang the players, the trophy still being passed amongst them.

And then there was a knock on the changing room door and a representative from Phone Valve came in to offer his warmest congratulations and to remind them that their victory had just earned them a very large pot of extra sponsorship cash from his company. This was met by a whole new round of screaming and shouting, and the man's hand was squeezed almost to a pulp.

A few months ago Rangers faced financial ruin. Now things were looking up. How fortunes could change!

After the Phone Valve man left, there was more singing and chanting, and Nat could feel his voice going hoarse on account of his vocal efforts. But he didn't care. He'd played a part in the club's history and hopefully not just today's fans, but fans in the future would get to hear of his and his teammates' exploits tonight.

A few minutes later, there was another knock on the door. Stan Evans stepped out and when he came back, he informed Fox that Helen Aldershot was waiting for him to attend a post-match press conference.

"Tell her I'll be a couple of minutes!" called the boss. He then bade everyone sit down, and took a long look round the room at the exultant faces.

"Well, well, well," he said softly. "Three months ago if anyone had told me we'd be where we are right now, I'd have bitten their head off for taking the mickey. But I look at all of you and I know tonight is real. I am proud to serve as manager of this club and I am proud of every single one of you. You were lions out there tonight. The match had everything, but you conducted yourselves with the utmost professionalism and you are a credit to Hatton Rangers Football Club."

He stared for a few seconds at the silver trophy, currently being held by Graham Dalston.

"I know it's not the Premier League or the FA Cup, but for all of us in this room, this is a massive deal – a gigantic feat. I want to thank you all for the commitment you've shown, not just this week, but throughout the last few months, through the dark days when relegation had us by the collar. I'm delighted for all of you and your families, and for everyone connected with this great club. Now, if you'll excuse me for a moment, I have a press conference to attend."

As the Rangers manager stopped speaking, there was a cacophonous outburst of applause from his players and Nat spotted tears in the eyes of Pierre Sacrois and Andy Young.

"We can watch him!" shouted Stan Evans, flicking a switch on a television at the side of the room and pushing it out so it took centre stage.

A Spanish sports presenter was talking to camera and replaying highlights of the final, including Nat's goals, both of which got a massive cheer from his teammates. And then it was off to a small room flanked by glass windows. A minute later, Ian Fox walked in and sat down at a table in front of several microphones. It was amazing nowadays how many sports channels there were, and the fact that every single game and tournament attracted media attention.

A question was shouted out in Spanish and a Talorca club official translated for the Rangers manager. "How much did you enjoy tonight?"

"It was alright, I suppose," replied Fox, deadpan, before his face creased into a smile. "No, to be truthful, I loved it! To win a trophy at a tournament containing such fine teams is a real achievement for any club."

The next question came in. "This is the first piece of silverware in your club's history. What do you plan on winning next?"

"The Champions League!" replied Fox. "But joking aside, I'd be delighted with a top ten finish in the Premier League."

"No disrespect to your club, Mr Fox, but did you believe before the game that you could beat a side as big as Talorca?"

"I think that *is* disrespectful," scolded Fox, in a mock-teacher voice. "Just because we don't have the financial resources of an Arsenal or a Barcelona, doesn't mean that we can't compete at the highest level. I think we showed tonight that good organisation and planning, and massive commitment from players, are what win games."

"Did you support your team withdrawing from the pitch after the racist behaviour of a section of the crowd?"

"If you'd seen my reaction on the touchline, you'd know that I supported them one hundred per cent, as did the Talorca manager and many of the Talorca team. I'll be very interested to see the referee's match report and how FIFA respond to this disgraceful incident. There's absolutely no room in football for these kinds of hateful people. They should be weeded out and kept a million miles away from any football match."

Nat and the rest of the changing room yelled their approval.

"How did you think Nat Dixon played tonight, and is he a big part in your future plans?"

"Dixon did well tonight," replied Fox.

There was an enormous cry of disbelief in the changing room.

"What's he on about?" laughed Emi incredulously. "Nat won us the game!"

"He's a very young player," went on Fox. "He's only at the very beginning of his career and he still has a mountain to climb before he's a settled player. He did show several sparks of brilliance, but I want to emphasise that tonight's was a first class *team* performance, and that all of my players deserve this trophy. It was their hard work that won it."

Cheers erupted in the changing room.

"Do you think your victory will mean you'll have an easier ride in the new Premier League season?"

"Football is a competitive sport," sighed Fox, "particularly in England. There is never an easy ride in the Premier League. Ask any foreign player in our league about our game and they will tell you that when they first arrive they are shocked by the ferocity. Up there with La Liga and Serie A, it's the best league in Europe. We're delighted to win here tonight, but when we return to

The families of the two finalists were invited to attend.

"I probably won't have a chance because I've got some paperwork to do for this job and I need to email it to the guy who's in charge. I'll see you there."

"When's your flight?"

"I tried to get on the team one with you, but there's no space, so I'm getting the 5.10. Well done again, mate. You were superb!"

"OK, everyone!" called Stan Evans. "You'll all have plenty of time to see each other tomorrow. We need to be heading back now!"

After more hugs, kisses and tears, the players clambered onto the coach.

The journey to the hotel was raucous and when they arrived back, the staff had hung up a huge sign over the front entrance:

CONGRATULATIONS TO OUR GUESTS – TOURNAMENT WINNERS, HATTON RANGERS FC!

It was a nice touch and the players appreciated it.

Fox limited the players to a couple of drinks, but Adilson – who didn't drink – and Andy Young, who hated alcohol, joined Nat in an apple juice. There was a piano in the hotel lobby and Pierre Sacrois amazed everyone by rattling off some show tunes, which everyone sang along to.

The other hotel guests, most of whom had no idea who Hatton Rangers were or what they'd achieved that night, were either intrigued by what was going on or thought it too loud and retreated to their rooms. At midnight the hotel manager approached them apologetically and asked them to curtail their celebrations. Evans and Fox stepped forward and said of course they would ensure that the riotousness stopped. And it did. Ian Fox's inner disciplinarian re-emerged and he told his players that sleep awaited them, because they had a formal lunch the next day, and in a couple of days time they'd be back in full training.

There were groans all round but, led by the Wildman, the players accepted this ruling. Cabs were called for Nat, Emi and Kelvin and the party broke up. Stan Evans went round, handing everyone their ID cards for Victor Mabena's lunch the next day. No pass, no entry. Nat tucked his into his trouser pocket. He then got massive hugs from everyone, before getting into his cab and driving off into the night.

Inés was in the kitchen and she stood up the minute Nat walked in.

"WELL DONE!" she beamed. "What a great match! And what brilliant goals! I've made you something to celebrate."

There on the table stood the most exquisite-looking chocolate cake.

"You didn't need to do this," Nat said, but he couldn't hide his delight.

"I know I didn't," she laughed, "but when you win something, you celebrate!"

She cut him a big slice and a smaller one for herself and

they stood there eating. It was one of the best cakes Nat had ever tasted.

"So, it's back to England tomorrow," said Inés.

"Yeah," sighed Nat, "we've got Victor Mabena's lunch with the Talorca players and our families – my dad will be there. It'll be interesting seeing Tieras again. I've got no idea how he'll be with his own players, let alone us. And then it's the flight home."

"Are you training on Monday?"

"No, the boss has given us a day off, but then it's straight back into it."

"He's a hard taskmaster, then?"

Nat thought about Fox's behaviour tonight and smiled. "He's old-fashioned, but he's a good man."

"Well, congratulations again. I'm so pleased for you."

A thought suddenly struck Nat – a question had been bugging him all week and even though it was a painful subject he wanted to know the answer. "Inés . . . do you mind me asking you something?"

"Not at all."

"Why do you keep the smashed motorbike in your shed. Isn't it a constant reminder of the crash? Doesn't it upset you?"

"I don't understand," replied Inés.

"The motorbike – the one your husband and José crashed on?"

"José and my husband didn't crash on that motorbike," replied Inés. "It's mine from years ago. I crashed into a fence and have never got round to fixing it."

"Oh," frowned Nat, "I thought that. . ."

"They were in a *coach* crash," explained Inés. "My husband was employed as a driver for Talorca FC. He worked for them for many years. He and José were completing the last leg of a journey when the coach swerved off the road and smashed head-on into a tree. My husband was killed instantly. José's leg was broken, but thankfully his life was spared."

"Right," nodded Nat slowly, realising how wrong he'd been. "I'm sorry I asked"

"I didn't want to fill you in on the details," said Inés, "but as you asked, that's the answer."

Nat took a breath and blew out his cheeks. "Well, thanks for everything, Inés. You've been a great host and I've really enjoyed it here. You've been amazing to me."

"It's a pleasure!" smiled Inés. "Will I see you tomorrow?"

"I'll spend the morning here and then go to the lunch at La Plaza. I'll take my bags because we're going straight from the stadium to the airport."

"OK. I'll be around until about eleven when I'm going to walk over to some friends. So I'm sure we'll get a chance to say goodbye."

As Nat walked to his room, he thought about the coach crash that had killed Inés's husband and shattered José's football career. That was all it took – one piece of bad luck and your life could be ruined.

He walked into his bedroom and shut the door. It was only then that he realised how completely exhausted he was. It wasn't just tonight's action on the football field. It was everything that had happened since he'd been here – the training sessions, the spat with Tieras at the radio station, José's possible involvement with car theft, the man he was convinced was stalking him, the Ray Swinton blackmail incident, the Celtic and Lazio matches and now the incredible final. How was it possible that so much could been packed into such a short space of time?

As he lay down, he began replaying the final in his head. He glossed over most of it and focused on his goals. He could see the build-up, his position, where everyone else was and then his two strikes. Seeing the ball beat Xavier Bergas and nestle in the Talorca net had been sweet the first time – seeing it twice had been outrageous!

He re-spooled through the goals again and as he did so, it hit him that Hatton Rangers fans back in England and all over the globe would be celebrating right now. And he'd made the victory possible. After all of those years on the road with his dad, following the ups and more frequent downs of Hatton Rangers's performances, here he was, providing other people with a night to remember.

Maybe winning the cup *would* inspire Rangers to a better Premier League season. How much of a part would he play in that season? Just because he'd scored twice tonight in no way meant that he'd be an automatic choice for Ian Fox. And then, of course, there was always the worry that someone would uncover his real age and spill the beans to the world. Nat thought once more about how complex his life had become over the last few months.

Finally, at about 2 a.m., all reconstructions of goals and shots and passes, and all other matters of significance in the brain of Nat Dixon, were switched off and he fell asleep.

Chapter 39
A Shocking Discovery

He was woken in the middle of the night by a sound in his room. He opened his bleary eyes and, in the darkness, saw a figure crouching down on the floor near the cupboard. He sat up quickly.

"Sorry." It was José's voice. "I left some batteries in here. Ah, got them. Thanks."

A second later, José was gone. Nat shrugged and went back asleep.

When he next woke it was 10.55 a.m. and Inés was peering round his door, asking if he wanted anything. He said he was fine and he got out of bed.

"I'm off to my friend's now, so I guess it's goodbye," she smiled.

She gave him a hug and kissed him on both cheeks. "I'm sure we'll see each other again at some stage," she grinned. "Now, go back to bed, but don't oversleep and miss that lunch!"

Having said his goodbyes, Nat rolled back under the covers, and the next time he checked his watch it was 11.48. He got out of bed and wandered into the kitchen.

As a child, JONNY ZUCKER devoured any stories about football or footballers, and was especially influenced by a book called *Goalkeepers are Different* by Brian Glanville. He set his heart on being a writer and, in particular, writing a novel that combined a football story with a thriller plot. *Striker Boy* is that book and *Striker Boy Kicks Out* is the sequel.

On the path to becoming a writer, Jonny has worked as a primary school teacher, FA qualified football coach and stand up comedian. A tiny part of him still believes he has a chance of making it as a professional footballer. Jonny lives in north London with his wife and three sons.

José was nowhere to be seen and Inés's laptop was on the table. He sat down in front of the screen and started using Google to try and find some information about the coach crash José and his father had been in. Ten minutes was wasted in fruitless searches, and then Inés's computer crashed. Finally, when the computer was up and running again, he unearthed a nine-month old article in the English-language magazine, *World of Business Affairs*. Entitled 'Spanish Transport Magnate in the Dock', it read:

Spanish multi-millionaire Victor Mabena, owner of the Mabena Vehicle chain, appeared in a Seville court yesterday, answering questions under oath about two recent crashes involving coaches manufactured by his company. The first coach ended up in a ditch, but thankfully no one was badly hurt. The second coach, however, was involved in a serious crash on a major road. This vehicle was being used by Talorca FC, the Spanish football club of which Mabena is President. The vehicle crashed into a tree and resulted in the death of one of the club's long-standing drivers.

Two independent experts gave evidence last week. The first expert, Maria Santos, acting for Mabena, claimed that the two crashes were both down to human error. She said that safety checks at Mabena's plant – where the coaches are produced – were over and above the national minimum safety requirements, and that the company was in no way to blame. She said that an

internal and thorough investigation had found absolutely nothing wrong with the coaches' braking systems. The company claim that, when they recalled the entire fleet after the crashes, no such problems were found on any of the recalled vehicles.

However, Daniel Malvades, acting for the family of the deceased man Frederico Mancini, insisted that both crashes occurred due to lax health and safety procedures at Mabena's plant. He pointed out that an independent safety check just three months prior to the crash had found several areas of weakness in the safety protocols at the plant, and claimed that these weaknesses led to the possibility of poor braking facilities in this specific model of coach.

Into this fray stepped Mr Mabena, who was calm and focused when answering questions. He stated that: "Safety at my plants is our number one concern. No stone is left unturned as we carry out a battery of tests on every vehicle. I, personally, would never, ever compromise on safety, and it is impossible for a coach to leave our plant unless it is in perfect condition. Once again, I offer my sincere condolences to Mr Mancini's family."

Nat's eyes widened as he read the piece. Not only had José and his father been in a coach crash, they'd been in a crash on a coach made by Victor Mabena's company. And there was obviously a lot of controversy about safety concerns surrounding that particular type of coach. It explained José's feelings about Mabena. José must believe that Victor Mabena and his company were responsible

But there was no sign of it anywhere.

And then something occurred to Nat. He'd woken up in the middle of the night and seen José crouching down in his room. What if José had lied to him and hadn't been looking for batteries? What if he'd been looking for Nat's ID pass? Was that possible? And then another thought hit Nat, but this one was more worrying. What if it wasn't a car theft that José was planning, but something else? What if he'd planned something to brutally avenge the death of his father? Nat suddenly shivered. This could potentially be very dangerous.

He quickly shoved his things into his bag, hurried into the corridor and stepped outside.

The jeep wasn't there. But Inés's small Fiat was. Nat bit his bottom lip. Walking to the main road and waiting for a bus might take ages. He hesitated for a few seconds and then ran back into the villa and grabbed the Fiat's keys off the work surface in the kitchen. He knew he was being impulsive and crazy, but something within him told him he had to act. He looked back at the villa for a second and then jumped into the car.

Nat had known how to drive since the age of ten. A bed and breakfast owner in Holland had taught him in a Mini in his huge backyard.

Nat turned the Fiat key, the engine purred and he headed up the hill, down the other side and spilled out onto the main road. His heart was pounding madly. It was now 1.32 – Mabena's event was thirty-two minutes old. Was he too late to prevent whatever it was that José was planning? Nat put his foot down and the Fiat's engine roared. He reached one hundred kilometres per hour, but that seemed to be as far as the engine would stretch.

Can't this car go any faster?

With the clock indicating 1.55, Nat swerved round the corner and the La Plaza Stadium came into view. He pulled up in one of the public parking spaces and saw that José's jeep was parked a short way up ahead. Nat felt his stomach twist, leapt out of the Fiat and sprinted towards the front entrance of the stadium. He was met by two burly security guards in black suits, brandishing walkie-talkies.

One of them said something in Spanish.

"I'm Nat Dixon!" he blurted out. "I'm a Hatton Rangers player. I need to get inside!"

"Where is . . . your . . . your . . . ID pass?" asked the first guard, in faltering English.

"I don't have it!" Nat responded. "But please let me in!"

The guards exchanged a look. Nat quickly reached in his jacket pocket for his mobile. It wasn't there. It must have dropped out when he was frantically getting his stuff together on leaving Inés's place.

"Please!" Nat beseeched them. "I played in the final last night. I scored both goals. I *have* to get inside!"

"No pass, no entry!" said the guard.

"Just call Mr Mabena or one of his team!" cried Nat. "They'll know who I am. I need to go in. I think . . . I think . . . something bad, really bad, could be happening in there. PLEASE!"

They looked at him with disbelieving eyes. Nat groaned.

Not only do they not recognise me, they think I'm some sort of chancer-kid, trying to blag my way inside!

"Sorry," said the second guard, "but it is a private event inside. You need to go."

Chapter 40
The Truth Dawns

With an increasing sense of foreboding, Nat turned and ran. He sprinted past the front facade of the stadium and turned left onto a long road beside it. The stadium was now on his left – on the right was a very long, modern five-storey office block. At the end of the road was a high metal gate with spikes on top, which led to the Talorca club car park – the place where the players, manager and club president parked their cars. Victor Mabena's car would be inside there.

Nat stood with his hands on his hips, panting, unsure what to do.

And that's when he spotted it. At the far end of the street, some scaffolding was attached to the office block. He looked both ways. There was no one around. So he started to run.

He reached the scaffolding, jumped up, caught one of the metal bars and pulled himself on. Then he began to climb.

Luckily it was a Sunday, so there was no one working inside the office block and therefore no one to see him climbing up this metal skeleton. At the top was a narrow wooden platform that went right around the building, giving access to all four sides. Nat began his ascent, but even though he was sweating profusely, progress was slow as he needed a new grip at each intersection.

When he reached the wooden platform, he climbed up one more section so that he was balancing on the very top metal bar of the scaffolding. His body swayed and he told himself not to look down. Without thinking about the consequences if he fell, he launched himself through the air and landed with a thud on a flat roof on the opposite building – La Plaza Stadium.

Now he had to get inside. He scanned the roof and saw a door in front of him. He tried it but it was locked. He hurried over the concrete, desperately looking for a way in. He passed sets of aerials and electrical pylons until he finally spied a chance. There was a large air vent tacked to a brick wall. It was old and rusty and Nat grabbed at it. At first it didn't give, but on his fourth yank, he pulled it off.

He looked through it and saw a short narrow tunnel. Kneeling down, he pushed the upper part of his body through the gap, followed by his legs. It was a tight squeeze, but he fitted in with a tiny bit of space to spare. Crawling was desperately slow and it took him a full ten minutes to reach the end, after which he lowered himself out, managing to swing his body round so that his legs hit the floor first. He was in a tiny square room with some brooms and mops stacked against one wall. Thankfully the door was open, and he walked out into a long corridor that stretched in both directions, with doors on either side of it. He turned right and ran, reaching a downward flight of stairs at the end. He raced down this flight and then another two flights, until he found himself on the ground floor. He stopped in front of a large white plaque on the wall with directions to various parts of the stadium. One of them had a crossed knife and fork beside it.

The Banqueting Suite! He'd seen it on José's plans.

He raced along the corridor and passed the kitchens, from which delicious smells wafted out. At the end of the corridor he saw two large wooden doors with glass portholes. He ran up and peered through one of these.

Inside was a large horseshoe of tables, at which sat the entire Hatton Rangers and Talorca parties. He spotted his dad sitting next to Emi and Kelvin. Ian Fox was beside Velasquez, the Talorca manager. Tieras was there with one of his kids – a girl aged about three – jumping up and down on his lap. In the middle of the front table, Victor Mabena had obviously just made some kind of speech because everyone was clapping and he was waving his arms to acknowledge them. He then made for a door at the far side of the room with the two henchman Nat had seen at the El Mar Stadium.

Mabena was on his way out. Nat had to find José.

He sprinted on down the corridor until he came to a lift. He looked at the numbers above it. There were six floors. He studied the sign and one word hit him.

Quinto. Fifth.

He'd also seen that – this time on one of the technical

drawings in José's hideout. He hit the button to call the lift. It seemed to take forever and as every second passed, his mind tried to predict what José was up to.

Finally there was a clunk and the lift doors slid smoothly open. As Nat ran inside and pressed number five, he heard someone shouting his name from a distance. But he had no time to stop and chat. He had to find out what was going on. The lift started making its way upwards. It reached the fifth floor and Nat sprang out. He was faced by yet another corridor and another set of doors on each side. These weren't locked. He flung each of them open. They were offices but they were all empty. At the end of the corridor was a door that had a steel bottom half and a glass top half. He ran towards it.

When he was nearly upon it, he froze. Through the top glass half he could see José inside. He was with another man, who looked like an older version of him. José was holding a black metal panel that looked a bit like a TV remote in his hand. It had wires coming out of one end.

What on earth is that?

Nat took another couple of steps and watched as José and his friend walked towards a huge floor-to-ceiling window at the far side of the room and looked out. Nat followed their gaze. The window looked down onto the executive car park five floors below. Victor Mabena was striding towards his black Mercedes – his two assistants at his side.

Nat looked from Mabena to the panel with wires and back again.

And that's when it hit him like a powerful punch in the face.

Mabena.

The coach crash.

Mabena's executive car.

José believed Mabena's lax safety regime had led to the coach crash that killed his father and left his football career in tatters. His father had been killed in one of Mabena's vehicles. Mabena had been spared any punishment by the courts.

It wasn't car theft José and his accomplice were going to carry out. They'd placed a bomb underneath Victor Mabena's car and they were about to set it off! The black panel in José's hand was the detonation unit.

Nat threw open the door and raced towards them.

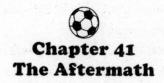

Chapter 41
The Aftermath

Nat saw through the window that Mabena had nearly reached his car.

José and the other man heard Nat's footsteps and span round.

"It's DIXON!" screamed José in Spanish. "The football player from the villa!"

"Get him, Rudy!" shouted the other man.

Nat had no time to ask why he had called José by another name, because José pressed a button on the panel, threw it over to his accomplice, and flew at Nat.

Nat's extra training with Stan Evans before the Celtic game came into instant use. He barged into José's shoulder with every ounce of momentum. José toppled and, as he fell, Nat kicked his bad leg for good measure. He knew it was a cruel thing to do, but the situation demanded it.

José let out a howl of pain and hit the floor. In the second Nat watched José fall, the other man pushed him in the chest. They both fell and, as he crashed down, Nat caught a glimpse of the panel.

Forty-two, forty-one, forty. . .

José must have activated the countdown. In less than a minute the bomb would go off! Mabena and the others would be blasted to smithereens!

The older man was now pinning Nat down on the floor, one hand on his throat, the other gripping the panel with a clenched fist.

Thirty-four, thirty-three, thirty-two. . .

Nat grabbed his hand with both of his own, but his strength was being sapped as his oxygen supply was being cut off.

Twenty-four, twenty-three, twenty-two. . .

The older man tightened his grip. Nat felt shooting pains of agony down his throat and in his chest. Four people were about to die.

Eighteen, seventeen, sixteen. . .

Nat threw his right arm out behind him across the carpet, frantically looking for something to grab hold of.

"That man killed our father!" shouted Nat's attacker. "Now it's his turn to die!"

Twelve, eleven, ten. . .

At that second, Nat's hand came into contact with something round and hard. It was a marble doorstop. It must have been knocked across the floor when he burst in. With incredible effort, he raised it above his head and smashed it against the side of the older man's face. With a scream, the man crashed off him, clutching his face in agony.

Eight, seven, six. . .

Nat jolted upwards and snatched the panel from the

here and then I burst in. Now will you tell me what's going on?"

Nat gave his dad a very quick résumé of what had just happened. He'd only just finished when two security guards from the club ran in and he had to explain the situation all over again, this time in slow English. They immediately made some calls and five minutes later the place was crawling with Spanish police officers. Mabena's car was contacted and was ordered to stop while the bomb squad arrived and took care of the device fitted to its underside. One of the officers on the fifth floor administered some first aid to the older man's cut head, and then he and José were handcuffed.

"He killed our father!" shouted José defiantly, as they were led away.

Following this, Nat was asked to give a statement to the police, but they had to wait until one of their number who spoke fluent English arrived. During the wait, Stan Evans and Ian Fox appeared, having been told the bare bones of what had taken place. They both looked at Nat in astonishment.

"Was getting into a scrape with Chris Webb not enough for you?" asked a disbelieving Fox.

"I didn't mean to get involved," replied Nat. "If I hadn't checked out the coach crash on the internet I would have never made the connection. It was when I discovered my ID pass was missing that I realised something might be up."

"Well, we're all glad that you did, son," said Fox gravely.

"Looks like you just saved four people's lives. Whatever those lads think of Mabena and his coaches, killing him and three others is not the right way to go about seeking justice. Just think of the agony it would have caused for *their* relatives."

"I can see where they were coming from," mused Nat. "I mean, José's career was destroyed by that crash *and* he lost his father, but I agree with you – murdering Mabena is way off the scale."

"Look, son, we need to head off," said Fox. "But we're not deserting you. Stan's going to get your flight changed so that you can travel home with your dad. I'll give you a ring tomorrow night – give you a day to recover and get your head straight, OK?"

"Yes, boss," nodded Nat.

The English-speaking officer then arrived, but before he could start interrogating Nat, Nat got in a question of his own.

"The guy working with José – do you know who he is?"

The officer nodded. "He is José's brother. He broke out of jail a few days ago, so it's doubly good you were here to do what you did."

José's brother. Why did Inés never mention him?

It was a full hour before the policeman had finished with Nat, by which time the team bus had already left for the airport.

Nat was delighted to be flying home with his dad rather than the rest of the squad. If he went with the lads they'd have a million questions for him and he didn't really feel like another full-on interrogation after the grilling he'd just had from the police.

The English-speaking officer thanked Nat and said he was now free to go. He warned him that the Spanish authorities would definitely need to speak to him again, but that this time it could be over the phone. He was fine to fly back to England, but would probably need to return to Spain when the case reached the courts.

A Talorca official then led Nat and Dave back downstairs and accompanied them to the front of the stadium, wishing them well on their journey home. They stepped out into the glaring sunlight and the first thing Nat saw was the red Fiat, parked pretty badly in one of the bays. In all of the mayhem he'd forgotten that he'd 'borrowed' it.

Standing next to the vehicle was Inés. Her eyes were red and blotchy – she'd clearly been crying. Nat swallowed hard and walked towards her.

Chapter 42
Wrapping Up

Nat quickly glanced at Dave and then at Inés again. How much did she know? Was she furious with him for getting involved? Did she hate him because he'd stopped her sons' plan and ensured they'd both go to prison for a very long time?

But as she reached him, she threw out her arms and gave him a huge hug.

"The police have told me everything," she said quietly, after she'd released him. "I knew José and his brother hated Mabena, but to try and kill him? This is something I cannot believe. You absolutely did the right thing, Nat. Your bravery stopped some bloodshed here and there are many people, including myself, who will always be grateful for what you did today."

There was silence for a few moments.

"Oh . . . sorry. . . Inés, this is my father, Dave."

They shook hands.

"Thanks for looking after my son so well," smiled Dave. "Sounds like you've been a fantastic host."

"It's been a pleasure," replied Inés softly. "It's terrible

that he found himself caught up in all of this."

There was another silence but before it became uncomfortable, something struck Nat.

"Inés, José's brother called him Rudy. Do you know why?"

"Rudy is his middle name," sighed Inés. "And Carlos is my other son's middle name. His real name is Fernando. They must have used their middle names because they wanted to avoid detection."

"Why haven't you mentioned Fernando to me?" asked Nat.

"Shortly after my husband was killed, Fernando started behaving very recklessly," said Inés sadly. "At first it was small things, but then he started hanging out with a group of very shady characters. I pleaded with him to drop them and stick to his old friends, but he didn't care about what I said any more. And then he started getting involved in criminal activity. On the first few occasions, I supported him, but then he and some 'friends' held up a store, and the owner was hurt in the process. When I heard that Fernando had been in the thick of it, I said I could not support him any longer and he warned me never to contact him again. When the case went to court, he was sentenced to six months in prison and I have not seen or heard from him since then, until the prison contacted me to tell me he had escaped. It looks now that he deliberately got sent to jail so that he could learn how to make bombs in prison – at least that's what one of the officers told me."

"I'm so sorry," said Dave.

"Their father is dead and gone," said Inés wistfully. "He is not coming back. They can't spend the rest of their lives trying to get rid of Victor Mabena. What's done is done. They must move on. Unfortunately, now they will both be spending a long time inside."

"Will you visit them?" asked Nat.

"José, yes. Fernando, I shall see how it goes."

They were all silent and then Dave spoke.

"Look, Inés," he said. "You've been a brilliant host to Nat. And now this terrible thing has happened to you. Nat tells me you're a teacher and that it's the middle of the school holidays now. Why don't you come to England for a bit, have a break? It would give you a chance to get away from here – have some time for yourself. We've got plenty of room and we'd stay out of your way if you liked. There's decent transport near us. You can get to central London in about forty-five minutes."

"That's a great idea!" said Nat enthusiastically.

Inés's face broke into a smile. "That is so kind of you, but surely you don't want a fussy Spanish woman to spoil your bachelor pad?"

"Nonsense!" said Dave. "We'd love it. What do you say?"

"It's a lovely thought, and I'm very tempted," she responded. "First, though, I'll need to find out a lot more about what happened here and what's going to happen to my boys. Perhaps, when the dust is settled in a few weeks, I will take up your kind offer."

"I understand," replied Dave, "but let us know.

You can come whenever you like for as long as you like."

"Thank you both very much," she replied. She shook Dave's hand, then grabbed Nat and gave him another rib-busting hug. "My famous football guest!" she laughed, pulling away. "It goes without saying that you are both welcome to stay with me whenever *you* want."

"We might need to!" grinned Nat. "Your cooking is miles better than his!"

"Easy now," cut in Dave, laughing.

Inés put out her right hand and at first Nat didn't know what she meant. But his gaze drifted over her shoulder to the Fiat and, with deep embarrassment, he handed her the keys.

"Er . . . sorry about borrowing the car without asking," he said sheepishly.

"You did what?" demanded Dave.

"It's no problem," she smiled. "In return, I have your mobile phone. It was on your bedroom floor." She handed it back.

"Thanks," said Nat.

"Now I'd better go," smiled Inés, "or I'll start crying."

She climbed into the Fiat, turned on the engine and pulled away.

"What are you going to tell your teammates?" asked Dave.

Nat shrugged his shoulders. "I have no idea. Like Ian Fox said, to be involved with one gang of criminals is one thing, to come across another is unreal."

"You're right there, mate. You've had enough

excitement in a few months than most people have in their entire lives."

"Shall we get a cab to the airport now?" asked Nat.

"Definitely," nodded Dave. "I'm just going to nip back into the stadium to use the toilet. I'll see you in a minute."

"Cool."

His father had just headed back inside when Nat saw a figure striding towards him.

It was the man – the stalker. Terror gripped him. If this guy was connected to Tanner he could be a psychopath too. He may have a gun. Nat shivered but he couldn't run.

The man reached him and dipped his right hand into his jacket pocket. Nat flinched. But instead of a gun, the man produced a business card.

Phil Gartside, Football Agent.

Nat looked at him in shock. "You're . . . you're an agent?"

"Is that so surprising?" replied Gartside. "I would imagine there are thousands of agents wanting to speak to you at the moment."

"Really?" said Nat.

"You're only sixteen and you won't be signing a professional contract with Hatton Rangers until your seventeenth birthday, right?"

Nat nodded.

"So I'm here to suggest an alternative direction for you."

"I don't understand."

"I represent several Spanish teams," explained Gartside.

"Spanish teams?" repeated Nat.

"Several clubs out here have been monitoring your progress, both in England and during your week in Spain."

"They've been following *me*?" asked Nat incredulously.

"Hatton Rangers is a good club to start your career," went on Gartside, "but with the talent you possess, there's a far bigger stage to parade what you can do."

"You're joking," mouthed Nat.

"I'm not joking," replied Gartside firmly. "The President and manager of one club in particular have made their position very clear to me. They're willing to offer you terms and conditions many light years away from what Rangers will put on the table."

Nat stood there, his mouth hanging open in astonishment. "Which club is it?" he heard himself ask.

"I represent the management team from Camp Nou, Nat," said Gartside. "They're deadly serious about signing you. They want you to play for Barcelona."

STRIKER BOY
Jonny Zucker

Nat Dixon is Premier League Football Club
Hatton Rangers's mystery new signing – and
their only chance of avoiding relegation.

It's every young footballer's dream come true,
and Nat feels as though he's fulfilling
his destiny. . .

But what his fellow players, the fans and
the press don't know is that Nat is only
thirteen years old. . .

**A thrilling story of one boy's plunge into
an incredible world of Premiership football
and deadly danger, that will have football fans
gripped from start to finish.**

BLACK AND WHITE
Rob Childs
Illustrated by John Williams

Josh is soccer-mad and can't wait to show off
his ball skills to his new classmates. After all,
he is the nephew of Ossie Williams –
the best footballer in the country.

Josh's arrival helps to give shy Matthew
more confidence, but it is not welcomed by
Rajesh, the school goalkeeper and captain.
With important seven-a-side tournaments
coming up, will the players be able to settle
their differences and work together
as a team?

DAN AND THE MUDMAN
Jonny Zucker

It is Dan's first day in his new school and already
he has had a run-in with Steve Fenton, the school
'tough guy'. In his last school it didn't matter
that Dan was Jewish – loads of his classmates were!
But here only Lucy is nice to him.

When Dan makes a mysterious clay figure for
his class presentation, he finds himself
back in time in the 16th century, where he encounters
the mystical Golem of Prague.

But little does Dan realise how his life will be thrown
into turmoil as he helps the Golem right wrongs that
happened many years ago.